Cath Crowley grew up in rural Victoria. She now lives in Melbourne and works as a writer and part-time teacher. This is her third novel.

Also by Cath Crowley

The Life and Times of Gracie Faltrain
Gracie Faltrain Gets it Right (Finally)
Chasing Charlie Duskin
Graffiti Moon
Words in Deep Blue
Take Three Girls

CATH CROWLEY

Gracie Faltrain takes control

Pan Macmillan Australia

First published in Australia 2006 in Pan by Pan Macmillan Pty Ltd
This Pan edition published in 2019 by Pan Macmillan Australia Pty Ltd
1 Market Street, Sydney, New South Wales, Australia, 2000

A catalogue record for this book is available from the National Library of Australia

Typeset in 11.5/15 pt Minion by Midland Typesetters
Printed by McPherson's Printing Group

The paper in this book is FSC® certified.
FSC® promotes environmentally responsible, socially beneficial and economically viable management of the world's forests.

To Charlotte, Dan, Declan, Ella, Esther and Tom Crowley.
More interesting characters than any I could make up.

Acknowledgements

Thank you Pan Macmillan, especially Anna McFarlane, Brianne Tunnicliffe and Karen Ward. Your warmth and insight have made this a much better book. Thank you also Anyez Lindop, for your support and fantastic sense of humour.

I could not write the character Gracie without all the people who gave up their time to teach me about soccer, especially Di, Dimitri, Natalie and Anna. Lastly, as always, thanks to my friends and family.

1

The most important thing in soccer is
teamwork. There's no better feeling than
killing the opposition. Together.
Gracie Faltrain

Flemming gives me a nod as small as a blink. Move an inch to the right, Faltrain, it says. So I move. And then I wait. Everyone on the field does. We're statues ready to fly into life as soon as Flemming sends his message to the ball.

'Give it to me,' I whisper. I want to take the shot so bad. I love the first Saturday in May. It's better than Christmas. Better than my birthday. It's our team's first official game of the season. And I want to make sure we win.

The sound of smacked leather echoes and I'm off. I soar past Shukman, the strongest player from the opposition, and keep the goal clearly in sight. It's so easy; I take a minute to play with the ball. I hook it onto my left ankle and toss it back to my right. Casual. Like I'm throwing it with my hands. I tease everyone on the field.

'Take the shot, Faltrain!' Martin yells all the way from goal. I run in close and slam it at the net.

'It's in!' Martin shouts. Of course it's in. I mean, come on. Gracie Faltrain kicked it.

I know what you're thinking. Gracie Faltrain is the same selfish player that she was at the end of last season. She's stealing the ball and hogging it so she can look like a star.

You're wrong. I've learnt my lesson. To play great soccer you have to be part of a team. Winning is a whole lot easier that way.

I still remember the feeling I had when we won the National Championships last year. Flemming took the kick and for a second no one was sure what would happen. The whole crowd held its breath while the sky held the ball. I knew Flemming wouldn't miss. He's an idiot sometimes, but he can play soccer. We wouldn't have won without him. You have to respect that.

'Faltrain, less dancing, more kicking,' Coach shouts at half time. Someone should read that guy the statistics on heart attacks.

'Did you hear me?' His words rip a layer of skin from my ears. Someone should read those stats to him, but it's not going to be me.

'He needs to relax,' I whisper to Martin.

'You never learn, do you, Faltrain.'

'What are you talking about?' I learn. I've learnt so much since last season I'm practically a whole new person. The Gracie Faltrain who played soccer like she was alone on the field? She's gone. I'm the new and improved Gracie. And she's going to have a great season. With the help of her team, she's going to win every game.

We run back onto the field and you know what? We do win. We win so big and I kick so good that Martin and Coach forget they were ever angry.

'How do you like that?' I say to Shukman on the way past.

I take a second to really love the look on his face. I slap hands with Flemming on the way over to Martin. Everyone was right, winning is so much better when the whole team helps. There's no better feeling than killing the opposition together.

'You were fantastic.' Martin leans in close and lines up rockets under my skin, ready to go. He kisses me and it's take-off time. Great soccer. Great boyfriend. Great life. Last season is far behind me. In the life and times of Gracie Faltrain, this year is going to be perfect.

2

Life's not just about winning, Faltrain.
Martin Knight

You think I don't know that?
Sometimes it's about evening
up the score.
Gracie Faltrain

Usually at the end of a season I have this flat feeling, like I've been flying for months and then all of a sudden someone cuts off my wings and leaves me grounded. You can play soccer for fun all you like, but hanging around in the back yard shooting the ball in the air can only keep things interesting for so long. It's the competition I love. And it's hard to win against yourself.

But after the Championships, we didn't have to go for months without a match. Coach signed us up for the off-season games. Most schools in the area play in them, but this was the first time we'd entered. 'Won't do you any harm to keep practising between seasons,' Coach said. 'Have a bit of fun competition.'

He had that last bit right. We had weeks of fun humiliating every team we played against. In most games the opposition didn't even get hold of the ball.

My favourite match was the one against Hayton High. It was a hot day, like playing soccer in an oven. I could feel my arms baking, slowly roasting me to gold. I felt good.

Dan Woodbury was the captain of their team. He won the toss and took the kick-off. That didn't matter to me; either way they were on the fast track to losing. Call it fate. Call it destiny. Call it Gracie Faltrain. As soon as the ball moved I was its new best friend. Woodbury stuffed up and kicked too high. I trapped it with my chest. Not my favourite tactic – a girl's got to think of her future – but necessary.

'Hello there,' I whispered to the ball, shifting it to the inside of my ankle. I hovered for a second, long enough to spot Flemming waiting near goal. Hot air rushed past me as I ran. The sun bit my face. I felt better than good. I felt great.

'Flemming,' I called, and flicked the ball to my knee. I bounced it high. I headed it. He kicked it. We scored.

'All right,' he shouted, and grabbed me round the neck. 'Give up now,' I heard him say to their goalkeeper, laughing as he walked off. Yep. Winning is a beautiful thing.

We won every game in the off-season competition. We played fast. We played hard. We played as a team. See? Told you I learnt my lesson. 'Nice try, Woodbury,' I said as I walked past him after the Hayton High match. 'Just nowhere near nice enough.'

You know the best thing about the off-season games, apart from the look on the other teams' faces? I proved that Gracie Faltrain is back. To stay.

I figure last year was a glitch. A hiccup. One missed kick in a long life of great soccer. The only bad thing about this year is that Jane, my best friend, still isn't back. She left with her family to live in England and it looks like they're staying. Jane's still on my side, though. She rang last night to wish me luck for the first match of the season. 'Got every game you're playing marked on the calendar,' she said.

'Thanks, Jane. I really love that you want me to do well.'

'Actually, Faltrain, I just really love being alive. I don't want a hit man turning up at my door.'

She's joking. She knows I can't afford a hit man on my pocket money. Anyway, if I had the money for a hit man, I'd use it on Annabelle Orion. Every chance she had last year, she made my life miserable. There's a long list of Annabelle offences, but there are three on the top of the chart. Number one: she made sure the whole school heard how I stuck my tongue in Nick Johnson's ear while I was trying to kiss him on our first and only date. (A freak accident. Usually my aim is perfect.) Number two: while the whole school was calling me Gracie-cotton-bud-Faltrain she put the moves on Nick. Number three: she loved every minute of it. They broke up over the summer and now she's seeing Dan Woodbury. So I won in the end. She keeps dating idiots. And I have Martin.

Annabelle still rates an eleven on a Richter hate scale of ten, though. She's rocketing off the scale this year because she makes it her job to hassle one of the best friends I have – Alyce Fuller.

I love Alyce, but let's be brutally honest, she's a walking target. She's the school nerd. She loves books and the library. She may as well wear a t-shirt that says 'Kick me' across the back in big red letters.

'Hey, Alyce,' Annabelle calls over the crowd today. 'Your boyfriend wants to say hi.' She points at the old man who cleans up after the game. 'Only one you're ever going to get.' Actually, Annabelle doesn't need the t-shirt. She kicks Alyce on instinct.

I give her the finger as she walks away. 'I could wipe the smile right off her face, Alyce, if you'd forget about your stupid rule and let me punch her.'

'It's not my rule, Gracie. There are these people called the police and a place called jail . . .'

'Whatever. No one would lock me up for taking out Annabelle Orion.'

'Gracie, please. Forget it.' Alyce says please like a kid begging for chocolate. She hates being noticed, especially when Andrew Flemming is standing close by. Alyce has it bad for the guy. She has it so bad her blood turns sweet when she sees him. Her cheeks are white as sugar. Her hands shake. She thinks I don't notice, but remember, I know the signs.

'Get changed, Faltrain,' Flemming calls. 'We're going out for pizza.'

'You want to come, Alyce?' I ask.

'I guess so.'

I know Alyce wishes Flemming had included her in the invitation, but to do that, he'd need to have remembered her name. Alyce can't have it both ways; she can't be Ms Invisible and still have Andrew Flemming know she's alive.

Alyce was great to me last year. She was there when I had no one else. One thing I've learnt? Don't forget the people who saved you. This year isn't just about Gracie Faltrain; I've got other plans, too. Alyce has played a losing game long enough. I want her mentioned by name on party invites, not stuck on at the end of mine as, 'Invite whoever else you like'. For that to happen, though, she has to change, because – last time I checked – reading and watching the news? Not high on the list of things that get you popular. Unless the people you want to party with are over fifty.

My job won't be easy. Alyce turns up for school every day looking like she got dressed in the dark. Last week I dragged her into my room and pushed one of my new shirts into her hands. 'Quick. Put this on and meet me out the front.' She shrugged and took the top. I know she only wore it to make me happy.

Alyce has no idea what it takes to be popular. You have to want it, sure. But you have to act like it's the last thing you want. It's a tricky business. Too much cool and you're a try-hard. Not enough and you're a nerd.

'Can't she just be herself?' Dad asked when I explained why Alyce needed to change.

'Dad, being yourself only works for a small, select group of people.'

The skin above his nose buckled into a frown. 'Why can't Alyce be a part of that group?'

Was the man wearing a blindfold? Was he delirious? Dad can't see Alyce's problem because he's exactly like her. His mind's always stuck halfway between here and the last page of a book.

'I've told you before, Dad. I don't make the rules. I play by them. Alyce can be herself later. When she's made it.'

Adults try to make things simple. They say stuff like, 'Go to the teacher if you're being bullied'. As if that'll help anything. I've seen kids ripped to pieces right in the middle of class. I did it to Alyce myself once, so I should know.

By the end of this season Flemming will call Alyce by name. I'll make sure of it. I'm making sure everyone does. Gracie Faltrain is back, Annabelle Orion. And this season is about evening up the score.

3

Score as many goals as you want for
Alyce, Gracie. She'll still be a loser.
She's best friends with you.
Annabelle Orion

I just wish the score wasn't so far in the other team's favour. Annabelle Orion and her mates are at least ten goals up. And Alyce is still in the change room.

It's a cruel twist of fate for Alyce that we have sport every Monday, period one. Ever tried to convince a parent that you're sick on the first day of the week? It takes dedication. It takes a good liar. And it takes about half the weekend, because you have to start lying by at least lunchtime on Sunday. Alyce has to turn up to school. She has to play sport. And what do both those things add up to for a nerd like her? Humiliation, to the power of about a thousand.

This term we're playing basketball. Alyce is even more crap at that than any other sport. Martin and I tried to give her a few lessons yesterday. 'Come on,' I said, dragging her off the couch and throwing her book to Martin. 'Don't give her that. No matter how hard she begs.'

'You just need a few tips,' I told her on the way to the court. 'And then it won't be so bad for you tomorrow.'

'Gracie, I don't care about basketball. I don't care about sport.'

'Look me in the eye and tell me that being picked last every single time doesn't bother you.'

'Being picked last every single time doesn't bother me, Gracie.'

'You're lying. I can see your eyes twitching.' I tossed her the ball. 'Now run towards the ring, and try to shoot.' It's a good idea to watch Alyce run through half-closed eyes. That way you're ready to block out the sight of blood.

There was blood, yesterday – just not hers. She threw the ball at the ring and almost broke Martin's nose. And he was standing behind her. At the other end of the court. 'I would have thought that shot was scientifically impossible,' he said, trying to make her feel better.

'Not really,' she answered. 'If you multiply the angle of the court by the distance and add me into the equation, it's kind of an algebraic certainty.'

'Don't worry, Alyce,' I say today. 'I'll make sure I'm picked as a captain. You can be on my team.' I stretch my hand up as high as it will go.

I should have known better. The rules of the universe clearly state: when you're desperate to be picked for something, forget it. The only time you can guarantee to be chosen at school is when you'd rather be hung out of a plane and dropped without a parachute.

'Andrew, you can be one captain and . . .' Mrs Tunnisi stops and looks around. 'Annabelle, you can be the other.' Great. Flemming will pick according to skill and Annabelle will pick according to dress sense. Either way, Alyce is stuffed.

Flemming chooses me first. It's painful to watch the crowd of kids sheltering Alyce slowly picked off till she's left without cover. If she could move quickly to a team, it wouldn't be so bad, but the rules are she has to wait until her name is called. And Annabelle Orion knows the rules.

Another thing I learnt last year: it's wrong to leave a person on the edges looking in. If Annabelle has a scratch of kindness on her, she'll call Alyce's name out quickly, make the end clean. Anything else is cruel.

But Annabelle Orion is cruel. I bet she plucked the wings off flies as a child. She waits five full seconds. I count.

I catch Annabelle's eye and mouth at her. 'Say her name. Say it.' She looks straight back at me and sighs, a sign to everyone that Alyce is worth nothing. 'Do I have to pick her?' she asks.

I want to hit her so bad. But I don't yell or look angry. I make myself as calm as sleep. Because there's something much, much better than getting mad. And that's getting Annabelle.

'Don't worry, Alyce,' I say while we wait for the game to start. 'She'll pay.'

'Gracie, it doesn't matter. It's not important.'

'Yes it is,' I answer. 'You're important.'

I'm not great at basketball. But I'm good. On the soccer field the ball belongs to me. Bought and paid for. On the court it's mine on loan and I'm a little behind in the payments. But I have speed. I have determination. And today I have what Annabelle Orion doesn't. I have the ball.

I shadow her the whole game. Every time someone passes I'm there first. I'm playing my own form of extreme sports – Extreme Orion Humiliation.

'She's not letting me have the ball,' Annabelle complains to the teacher halfway through.

'That's the point,' Mrs Tunnisi answers. 'She doesn't have to.'

I keep it up the whole game, even though there's a stitch sewn tight across my middle. Even though I'm sweating harder than Corelli, the worst player on our soccer team, on a bad day. I want to send Annabelle a message she can't miss: mess with Alyce, and you mess with me.

About five minutes before the end of the game Annabelle decides I'm not going to win without a fight. Someone passes to her and she starts running. I'm a step behind her the whole way. If she makes it, Alyce will have lost. I grit my teeth and slam my feet at the ground. She slams hers harder. I reach out to grab the ball but she's too quick. I trip and slide along the ground, collecting stones in my skin on the way.

Annabelle shoots at the ring. Everyone stops. I catch sight of Alyce, faded in the background while everyone else is colour. I find the last scrap of energy left in my legs and I leap. I'm in time to tap the ball once. It spins round the edges, licking the lip of the hoop. It circles twice. And drops out.

'And that,' Flemming says on the way off the court, 'is why I don't make Faltrain mad anymore.'

Annabelle snarls at me as I walk past. I wave back at her.

'No need to thank me,' I say to Alyce as we walk towards the change room. She gives me that funny little half smile of hers.

That's another reason my job this year won't be easy. Sometimes I wonder exactly what it would take to make Alyce Fuller really happy.

4

Mum used to say, 'Marty, good soccer
players can read their team-mates' minds.
They can anticipate their every move.'
But then my mum was never
around to meet Faltrain.
Martin Knight

'Heard about your basketball game today,' Martin says when I get to his place after school.

'Annabelle had it coming.'

'I reckon she did . . .'

I can hear the 'But . . .' dangling from his lips. 'But what, Martin? Say it.'

'You ever think maybe stuff like that doesn't help Alyce?'

'I humiliated Annabelle today. How's that not helping?'

'I reckon you need to let her stand up for herself, that's all.'

'She doesn't though. That's the thing. She lets Annabelle treat her like a loser.'

'From what I hear, Faltrain, people thought Alyce was a loser today for another reason besides Annabelle.'

'You mean I made her look like a loser? I helped her. Annabelle'll think twice before she lays into Alyce again.'

'That's not the way she works and you know it. Orion gives Alyce a hard time because she knows how much you hate it.'

'I do hate it. And you know what else I hate?'

'I have a feeling you're about to tell me.'

'You. And everyone else who stands back and lets Annabelle do whatever she likes to the little people.'

'Not so long ago you were picking on the little people yourself.'

'You think I'm like Annabelle Orion?'

'That's not what I said.'

'That's exactly what you said.' I turn my back on him.

'Come on, Faltrain. I was only trying to help.'

So was I, you idiot, I think as I walk away, but does anyone thank me?

I know what Martin would have done if he'd been there today – he'd have stood back like he always does. He's been different since we came home from the Championships. I thought we'd be closer this year but we're not. He's quiet; thinking about his mum all the time, and how she left them. No one in the Knight family talks about her leaving, not Martin's little sister, Karen, not his dad. I wonder sometimes if they all agreed to lock her memory out one day, or if it happened slowly, like a door closing and clicking shut.

A few months ago he and I watched this television show about a woman who'd left her family. Martin had the remote and I kept expecting him to switch the channel, but he didn't. He sat through it, right to the end.

After it'd finished I wanted to say something to make the air breathable again. It went into my mouth and clogged my lungs like wool. Martin's the only one who can make me feel like that. I worry about Mum and Dad, and Alyce and Jane, but I don't feel what they're feeling, like I do with Martin.

'Do you want to talk about it?' I asked.

'Talk about what?'

What did he think I meant, who was going to win the World Cup? 'Your mum, Martin.'

'I told you before, there's nothing to say.'

Call me crazy, but if my mum had left me, you can bet I'd have plenty to say. Like, why did she leave, and when did she think she'd be back, and was this some sort of midlife crisis like Dad had last year?

Martin barely talks about his mum at all, though. He says he doesn't need to. He reminds me of that movie about the cyclones, the one where the wind is spinning cows and cars in the air, and the people in the town think they're safe because all of a sudden everything's quiet.

Only they're not safe. Any idiot can see they're right in the middle of the storm. There's a huge cow coming their way and they're cooking dinner or taking the rubbish out. 'It's the unexpected cow that'll kill you,' Jane said after we'd watched it, and she was right. A storm like that only circles for so long. And then it hits, ripping everything in its way to ribbons.

The last time Martin really spoke about his mum was on the way back from the Championships. It was nearly night and I was sleepy and he talked so low I almost couldn't hear him over the hum of the engine. 'She loved soccer, Faltrain. She said the game reminded her of life. "People weaving in and out of each other, Marty, all looking to get the same thing, all desperate for it."'

'What are they desperate for?' I asked, but I fell asleep before he answered and I haven't asked him about it since. I thought on that bus ride that things would be better for Martin when he got back, but I don't think that they are. Mr Knight might be trying, but from what I can see, he's not trying hard enough.

Martin's different on the field, too. Even Coach can see it. He doesn't have the edge anymore, like he's sitting back and waiting for someone to give him the ball. 'You're playing like a girl,' I said to him in the off-season games.

'You'd want to watch who you're calling a girl, Faltrain,' he answered, and kept packing his stuff into his bag.

'You know what I mean. You've lost something out there.'

'And what's that, Faltrain?'

I didn't answer. I couldn't say he'd lost a part of himself. What good would that do unless I could tell him how to get it back? Martin's mum took a piece of him when she left all those years ago, but for a long time the hole in Martin was too small to see. For some reason this year it's getting bigger. And it doesn't look like his mum is coming back to mend it any time soon.

Coach made him switch positions with Maiden halfway through the off-season games, so now he's in goal. 'It's an important position, Knight,' Coach said when he announced it at practice, but we all knew. So did Martin. He's played soccer most of his life; he knows it's a comedown. Right from the start Martin has been the one everybody looks up to. He gets the ball and passes it so someone can take the perfect shot. He plays underneath the team, keeping it afloat.

At least he did.

'Goalie protects the team from attack, Faltrain,' he said to me the day Coach made the switch. 'It's a key position.' And he bent down to tighten his laces, even though they didn't need it.

It is, but not when you're stuck there because you're playing worse than Corelli.

'We can train together, Martin. Prove to Coach you should have your old position back,' I said on the way home that night.

'Faltrain, I told you, I want to be in goal. Just leave it.'

That's how most of our conversations end, these days. I try to talk to him and he says, 'Leave it, Faltrain'. But if he keeps leaving things all over the place and never bothers to pick them up, there'll be bits of him all over Melbourne. I'll only have half a boyfriend. If I'm going to have that, I want the half that passes to me in the midfield.

'Sometimes you have to wait until a person is ready to talk, baby,' Dad said when I told him about Martin.

'I don't want to wait. I want him to be as mad as I am that Coach stuck him in goal. Something happened after he got back from the Championships and I want to know what it is.'

'That's like reading the last page of a book first. Would you do that?'

'I always do that.'

Dad looked at me like I was a criminal. 'Gracie, the last page doesn't mean anything unless you know how the character arrived there. You have to let Martin tell his story in his own time. If you don't do that, you won't understand it, anyway.'

I understand that Martin's trapped in goal, like he's trapped every day. Sometimes he's cooking dinner for his dad and Karen and me and there are lines of shadow across his face, like I'm staring at him through the bars of a cage. I want to break it open and force him out. But it's his mum who has the key.

Even when he doesn't mention her, she's there in everything he does. She's in all the things he remembers about soccer. She's in his heart, and if he doesn't talk about her, she'll get too big to fit. She'll force her way. And that's when things will get messy.

I know because until I fixed things with Dad last year, I felt the same way. I thought about him all the time, how much I missed him. Everything good I did I imagined he was there watching. And everything bad that happened I wondered what he would say to make it better.

Things aren't perfect now that Dad's back. Sometimes he and Mum fight for days and days. And then sometimes they don't talk to each other at all. They think I don't notice how they stop speaking when I walk into the room, but I do. I see their arms folded across their chests and not around each other.

Last year, when Dad was away, he did something to change the weather in our house. Mum can be told a million times it isn't going to rain, but she always carries her umbrella. On those days when they fight I feel it in my bones; a winter ache, like wind slicing across me on the soccer field.

'Gracie, baby,' Dad said one time when it was really bad, 'we're fighting for the other person, not with them.'

'You're not leaving again, then?'

'I will never leave you. You're the only spot on the map worth visiting. It's hard for you to understand, I know, but your mum and I are arguing because we're scared. She's afraid I'll leave and I'm afraid she'll never trust me to stay.'

'So tell her that.'

'Hearing something and believing it are two different things. Your mother will trust me again, but she has to find her own way.'

'And what if that never happens?' I asked.

'It will.'

Dad's a big believer in fate. According to him, the two of them were destined to be together because Mum hit him in the nuts with a tennis ball.

'Your dad has confused fate with tragedy, Faltrain,' Jane says.

'I hit him in the balls on purpose,' Mum says.

'Whether she hit him there on purpose or not,' Alyce says, 'their love could still be predetermined.'

I'm on Mum's side. Fate needs a little help sometimes, and if she was the one to get things started, then Dad has every right to get in there and give it some help to keep it rolling. I figure it's time he started lobbing some balls in her direction, you know, hit her with some good times, remind her about their beginning, when they first started dating.

If he does that, then Mum might start to tust him again like I do. Having dad back makes me feel warm and safe, like being inside on a night when the windows are full of frost.

I want Martin to feel that way, too.

'Faltrain,' he said when I explained it to him, 'my parents are different. Mum doesn't love Dad anymore.'

'I wasn't saying they should get back together. I meant that if your mum's not here she can't fix things with you.'

'She stopped loving me as well,' he said, and I could tell he believed it.

'How can that be?' It was like saying there wouldn't be a sun when we woke up in the morning. He pushed his hands further into his pockets and shrugged. 'It just is,' he said. And after that he walked a little faster.

It doesn't make me feel better, getting angry at him tonight. Apart from winning at soccer, there are only two other real buzzes I get, ones that make my blood hot like I've kicked a goal. Martin's smile. Martin's kiss.

'Well, Faltrain,' as Jane would say, 'there's no way you're scoring a goal tonight.'

'Mum,' I ask when I get home, 'would a mother ever stop loving her kid?'

'Is this a question about you?'

'No. Martin, mainly.'

'I can't answer for his mum, love. Only she can do that.'

'Well you, then. Could you ever stop loving me?'

'Never, Gracie Faltrain. I will love you until I'm dead and buried. And then I'll love you from the grave.'

'How could Martin's mum leave him then?'

'Maybe she knew that if she stayed, she'd lose herself, and then there'd be nothing to give to Martin anyway.'

'But that could never happen to you, right?'

'That would never happen. Without you I am lost.'

'And Dad?'

She hesitates for just a second, but I see it in her eyes. 'He's lost without us, too.'

Dad and I are already toasty, but I guess Mum's taking a little longer to heat up. She'll trust him eventually, though. It's like when your feet are ice and you can't sleep. But then you wake up in the middle of the night and they're warm.

Mum and Dad are lost without each other, just like Martin is lost without his mum. I want to find a way to fix things for people this year. I want clear skies and sun and soccer. I want another winning season. For everyone.

5

The average goldfish has a memory of
approximately 3.65 seconds.
The International Journal of Scientists

Lately Martin acts like he doesn't care enough to remember our fights. He has the memory of a goldfish: gone after a few seconds. Even after our biggest arguments, I can call him and it's as though nothing happened. I never kicked him. Or punched him. Or called him an idiot.

I can't really complain; most times for me that's a positive, but once in a while it'd be good to get a little reaction. At least I don't have to worry about Martin breaking up with me. I'd only have to hang around for five minutes and he'd forget why he'd done it.

'Wait'll you hear the news, Faltrain,' he says at practice this afternoon.

'What?'

Coach walks out from the change room and starts yelling before Martin has a chance to answer. 'Right, team,' he shouts, moving backwards and forwards like a shark about to feed. 'I've got news. Big news.' He spreads his hands wide to show us the size he's talking about. My stomach twitches. The last time we had news that wide we entered the Championships. 'We're playing in the Firsts competition this year.'

My twitches are so big after he says that, it's like my insides are dancing. I can tell by the way everyone's shifting around that they feel the same. The Firsts is the top inter-school competition. We've never entered a team before. 'No point in entering if you're not good enough,' Martin told me a couple of years ago. 'You just end up looking stupid.'

'I'm putting together fifteen of the best players we have,' Coach goes on. 'Everyone in the school can try out for it. That means you need to be serious if you want to make it.'

'What happens if we don't get picked?' Corelli asks the million-dollar question. 'Do we still get to play soccer this season?'

'I want two teams. One to keep going at the level we are now. Another to play inter-school Firsts.' Everyone here knows what that means. If you don't make the Firsts then you're second best.

'I have to be on that team, Martin.'

He doesn't answer. His eyes are locked on Coach.

'Firsts season starts at the end of the month. This year the final is being televised,' Coach says. 'Talent scouts'll be there. If you're good enough you could get picked to represent the state.'

Okay. My whole body is twitching now. I feel like I've drunk fifty cups of coffee in a row. And I don't drink coffee.

'For the next two weeks I'm opening up practice to anyone in the school who wants a shot. After that there'll be tryout matches. I'll pick from those. Now drop and show me what you're worth. I want twenty push-ups.'

'I'll die if I don't make that team,' I say, forcing my shaking arms straight for the fifteenth time. I'm so excited I barely feel the pain. 'We're going to win the final on television. We'll get picked to play on the state team.'

'Pretty sure you'll make it, then?' Flemming asks.

'You just worry about yourself,' I answer. 'I know I'm good enough.'

'You think you're so good, Faltrain, give me twenty more push-ups after everyone's finished,' Coach yells. I might be excited, but I'm not insane. After forty push-ups, believe me, I feel it. I'm glad today that my boyfriend is a goldfish. He drops down beside me and gives Coach another twenty as well.

Martin and I stay on the field until the light fades. We chase circles around each other, stealing the ball and running for goal. He's playful tonight; he knows he can kick any way he wants and still make the shot. This is the Martin I love, so confident on the soccer field that he barely has to try. This is the Martin I want. He runs and all the sadness drops away. I'd give anything to keep him like this.

I race up beside him and kick the ball forwards. He looks surprised when I don't chase it. I catch him instead. Kiss him. I feel the blood rushing along my arms, flooding my skin. 'You didn't kick a goal, Faltrain,' he says.

'Yeah I did,' I tell him. And then I take the ball and fly.

I want to be training already, showing Coach and the rest of the team that I'm ready. It'll be the hardest competition I've been in yet. If I can make that team, I'll have proved I'm one of the best.

I can do it; I know I can. I'm better than all of the players in my school and most of the guys in the competition will be the ones we hammered in the off-season games. If Dan Woodbury is anything to go by, we'll be television champions by the end of the season. It'll be even better than winning the Championships.

Martin and I went along to a Firsts game, once. It was a couple of years ago. I could barely sit still. My feet kicked out as if I was the one taking the goal.

'You can't stand being in the crowd, can you?' He was right. I wanted to be out there proving how good I was. Me. A girl. Gracie Faltrain.

'I can play better than some of them,' I said to Martin that day.

'They're pretty big, Faltrain.'

'Soccer's about skill, not height.'

'I'm not talking about height.' He pointed at a kid who looked like he was a close relation of a brick wall. 'I'm talking about width.'

'I could take him. No problem.'

Martin's laugh bounced around the stand. 'I don't know if you could. But I would love to see you try.'

It's almost dark tonight by the time we stop playing. 'Come on,' he says. 'I have to be home in time to cook dinner.'

'About yesterday, Martin . . .'

'Forget it, Faltrain. It doesn't matter.'

Martin leaves me at my gate and jogs away. He's a shadow before the sound of his feet disappears. I know he hates to fight. I know that talking about his mum is hard. But if you keep saying that nothing matters, then sooner or later, nothing does.

When Coach talked about playing for the state today, Martin's eyes were wide and clear. Whatever has happened since he came back from the Championships, he has to face it. Maybe if we're picked for the state team, he'll have something to look forward to. Maybe he'll remember what it feels like to win.

6

Four equals a double date.
Every idiot knows that.
Andrew Flemming

'Faltrain, you're still kicking the ball too wide. You'll miss the goal like that,' Flemming yells from the edge of the field. He and Martin and I have scheduled in extra practice sessions every day before the tryouts.

'When have I ever missed a goal?' I ask.

'I can remember last season you missed a few.'

'That was different,' I say, and to prove it I run in close to Flemming and spin the ball near his feet. He moves to take it off me and I steal it back. 'What's that you were saying?' I yell, running, feet skimming grass.

'Knight, tell your girlfriend to stop showing off.'

Martin has already left the field, though. He's sitting at the edge talking to Alyce. She can't play sport, but she loves to watch. She comes to most matches, cheering in the crowd with my parents. Sometimes I look up into the seats and for a second, the faces blurring, I think it's Jane.

Alyce Fuller and I aren't exactly twins, Faltrain, Jane wrote when I emailed her that. She was right. She's nothing like

Alyce, except for one important point: both of them make me feel like I'm home. I can laugh so hard I almost wet my pants, and I can cry just as hard if I need to.

Alyce's hair falls over her eyes as she's talking to Martin. She wears it like a curtain, pulled across so people can't see the whole of her. I wish she'd throw back her head and laugh loudly like she does when she's alone with me. If boys could see her like that they'd be lining up in the street to ask her out.

'We're going to the movies tonight, me and Martin and Alyce,' I say as Flemming and I walk off the field. 'Want to come?'

I can see him hesitate and I feel like punching him. He's thinking two girls and two guys equals a double date. I can see pressure building in his brain. Don't try to add two and two, Flemming; you'll only end up hurting yourself.

'I've got homework,' he says, and starts running for his life. 'See you tomorrow, Knight,' he calls, and half waves to Alyce. For the second time this week, he doesn't even bother to say her name. This is going to be harder than I thought if a guy like Flemming would rather do homework than go to the movies.

'He's not coming?' Martin asks.

'I think he has to do some stuff for his dad.' Alyce doesn't need to hear that she rates below homework on the excitement scale. She picks up her books and keeps the curtain of hair pulled over her eyes. A person doesn't need a whole lot of imagination to see what the main show is, though: Disappointment, starring Alyce Fuller.

'It would never work,' Martin says while Alyce is in the bathroom before the movie starts.

'Why wouldn't it?'

'For one, because Flemming is a guy.'

'Isn't that a reason why it could work?'

'I mean he's a *guy* guy. He hangs with Annabelle's crowd.'

'I can take care of Annabelle.'

'He doesn't even read. What would the two of them talk about?'

'I've seen him with the sports pages. Anyway, what matters is that Alyce likes him.'

'Stay out of it, Faltrain. Let the two of them make their own decisions.'

If I did that, Alyce would spend every day in the library as part of the 'I Love Reading' club.

'Anyway,' Martin whispers, 'Flemming's too busy for dates.'

'Busy with what?'

'He's about five months behind on his schoolwork.'

'We've only been back four months.'

'Exactly. He's in serious trouble. His dad wants him off the team if he can't catch up.'

This is perfect. Flemming needs help in the homework department. Alyce runs that department.

'Did I miss anything?' Alyce asks as she sits down next to me.

'Nothing's started yet,' I say. 'But it's about to.'

Martin gives me a sharp kick in the leg. I kick him back. Double hard. The opening soundtrack drowns out his yelp. Don't mess with me, Martin. I know exactly what I'm doing. If Alyce wants Flemming, then it's Flemming she's going to get. Like I said before, in life, things don't happen by chance. They happen because you make them.

I mean, whoever organises fate must get pretty busy. And

quiet people like Alyce? They can't exactly be top of the list. Think about all the celebrities in the world. Why do they get the million-dollar destinies while the Alyce Fullers get nothing? Because they're louder. They're tougher. They don't take no for an answer. With Mum and Dad, fate needed a helping hand. When it comes to people like Alyce, it needs a kick.

I call Jane when I get home from the movies. Mum buys me a phone card every two months. 'Once it's spent, Gracie, that's it.' I figure I need a little Jane advice if I'm going to get the ball rolling with Alyce and Flemming.

'Have you actually asked her if she likes the guy?' Jane asks.

'No. But she never mentions him.'

'It's a crazy thought, Faltrain, but maybe Alyce never mentions him because she's not interested?'

'No way. She stares at his feet all the time.'

'Maybe she likes feet.'

'She doesn't stare at mine. Or Martin's. Only Flemming's.'

'You know, you're right. Feet are the windows to the soul. Imagine all those idiots out there staring into each other's eyes.'

'I just want her to be happy, Jane.'

'Does he stare at her feet?'

'Good question. I'll check.'

'People can hurt easily, Faltrain. There was this girl at school over here who had heaps of friends and now almost everyone's ignoring her . . .'

'What has that got to do with anything? Alyce doesn't even have any friends other than me, so I can't make things worse in that department.'

'I'm just saying be careful.'

'I will be, Jane.'

It's the first time in years that Jane and I have come close to snapping at each other. It feels strange because I don't know why.

'Well, I guess I'll talk to you soon,' she says, and hangs up. Jane has been overseas for ages now. But this is the first time I've felt like she was too far away to touch.

I sit in between Mum and Dad on the couch tonight. I stare past the TV, and try to remember what Jane looks like. I can picture her hair and the clothes she wore the day she left, but her face keeps disappearing.

'Something the matter, baby?' Dad asks.

'Not really. Jane was just acting sort of weird on the phone.'

'Weird?'

'Yeah. Kind of far away.'

'England is far away,' he says.

I guess it is. Jane just never made me feel like it before.

'Are you watching that DVD I rented?' I ask.

Dad nods. 'I think I've told you before, your mum and I saw this film on our first date.'

'You know I never listen to you, Dad,' I say, kissing him on the top of his head. 'I have homework to do.' I leave them alone so they can move closer on the couch.

It's like there's a fence between them. Dad's waiting for Mum to step across. It's getting smaller every day, so why not just reach out and pull her over? But he doesn't. He stays on his side and she stays on hers. And they talk across the fence like they're neighbours. Not like they had a first date, once, not like they kissed and then fell in love.

'Mum, can I work some more hours at the shop?' I ask when she comes in to kiss me goodnight. 'I need a little extra cash.'

'And why is that?'

'There's a dance coming up. I want a killer dress.' If Dad won't lob a few memories in Mum's direction then the plan is to do it myself. That's why I rented the DVD.

'This will be your and Martin's first social.'

'Yep. And I want to look hot.'

'Your dad took me to a dance on our second date. He bought me roses.'

Way to go, Dad. 'That was pretty romantic.'

'I thought so, until we stopped to pick up the couple we were double dating with. She was allergic. Her face swelled up like a tomato. We spent most of the night in the casualty department. Your dad thought we were bad luck as a couple. The first time we met I hit him in the balls during tennis and by the third date he'd put my friend in hospital.'

'But he asked you out again?'

'I asked him, Gracie. Remember, you're my daughter.'

'What happened on the fourth date?'

'We kissed. And there was no going back.'

'I wonder if Dad remembers.'

'You know he does.' Mum looks at me with her hands on her hips. 'He told you the story yesterday when you asked him where Martin could rent a suit.' She looks at me accusingly. 'I think that's what they call "busted", isn't it?'

'Pretty much.'

'Gracie, I know you want your dad and me to be exactly the same as we were before, but some things take time.'

'How much time?'

'I'm not a train, Gracie. I don't have an estimated minute of arrival.' She runs a finger down my cheek and the roughness of her skin makes my face tingle.

'Do you remember last winter when you helped me in the nursery? We had to cut back all the plants. I told you that some trees need to be pruned right to the base, or they'll never grow again.'

'You let me have the clippers because you said the harder the plants were ripped back, the better it was.'

Mum laughs. 'They grow so much better for the cutting. When you were young, you followed me around, yelling at me when I chopped off all the growth. You collected the flowers after they fell. I told you that if we didn't cut them, they'd never be green again, just thick and wooden like the old lavender bushes that you hated.'

'You said that once lavender got like that, it may as well be torn out.'

'Your dad and I aren't lavender, Gracie.' She smiles. 'I promise you. We're magnolia: the first things to come back in the spring.'

'You're saying that you and Dad will be all right in four months, then?'

'I'm saying be patient. Most things have to sleep awhile at some time in their lives.'

Whenever Mum sliced the garden back to its bones she always said the same thing: 'Winter will end. And there will be green like you've never seen before.'

I know she's right. I have to trust her. But it's the hardest thing to imagine that the garden will look good again, when the trees are as empty as clothes hangers. And their leaves are lying all over the ground.

7

1. Do not distract or startle
other students when conducting experiments.
2. Know the locations of all safety
equipment. Know where the fire alarm
and the exits are located.
Science Safety Manual

Mum's a bit more Zen now that she's older. Where was her patience and her talk of magnolia when she was smashing that tennis ball at Dad? I guess what she means is that once the love ball is rolling, so to speak, then it's okay to sit back and wait.

That's what I'll do with Alyce and Flemming. I'll turn up the heat a little, give them a bit of time together, and see if they mix. And if they don't? I'll back off. They'll go their separate ways. No harm done.

'Gracie, are you listening to Mrs Turner?' Alyce asks. 'She said this experiment is very delicate. That chemical needs to be handled carefully.'

'What, this blue stuff?' I give it a bit of a shake. 'Looks safe enough to me.'

'That's what Jamie Duper said last year.'

I put the beaker down and my goggles on. Jamie Duper has no eyebrows. 'So, Alyce, what do you think about Flemming?'

'What? He's a nice boy, I guess.'

A nice boy? Were you born thirty-five years old?

'Gracie, you need to light the Bunsen burner and heat the liquid in your beaker before I pour this in a bit at a time.'

I add some heat; turn the flame up to high. 'So, he's just nice?'

'Gracie, someone will hear you.' She's getting flustered. That's a definite sign, right up there with sugar in the blood. Her goggles are fogging up. Her cheeks are red. Her hair is bunched up at the sides of her face so she looks like a scared rabbit.

'I think you like him.'

'What?' she says, loud enough for Mrs Turner to tell us to be quiet. 'I don't like him.' She lowers her voice and pours all of the blue stuff into the beaker.

'Uh, Alyce,' I say.

'You haven't said anything about this to anyone else, have you?'

'No. Uh, Alyce . . .'

'Because I don't like him.'

'Alyce, is that thing meant to be smoking?'

'What? I can't see anything with these things on.' She pulls off her goggles. 'Oh, this is definitely not good.'

And there's the difference between Alyce and me. I would have said something like, 'Run!'

'Alyce, don't stand there, run!' I yell at her. Our beaker is spewing out blue liquid like a 7-Eleven slurpy machine gone crazy. Alyce is mesmerised by her monster creation. I'm hopeless at science but, like most kids, I know a little something about slurpy damage control. When the machine has gone crazy, and the man behind the counter is looking at you as if to say, 'You're paying for everything that thing is pumping out', there's only one rule to follow. Dump that cup and cut your losses. Everyone knows it. Except Alyce. I bet she goes to the counter and pays for every chunk of ice wasted.

'Everyone remain calm, no one knock the Bunsen burners,' Mrs Turner keeps calling. No one's listening. The number one rule of classroom behaviour: if you get the chance to scream and run, you do.

'I've never made a mistake with an experiment before,' Alyce says.

'I know. It's fantastic.' You get a sign like this, and fate's definitely giving you the big thumbs-up.

Alyce could make worse choices. Flemming plays a good game of soccer. His left foot is stronger than his right, but we can work on that. I don't see any reason why the two of them shouldn't hit it off. There's the Annabelle problem of course. But there was the Annabelle problem with Nick and me. And didn't that end well, Faltrain? I ignore Jane's voice in my head. I'll just make sure Alyce knows how to kiss before I send her out on a date. Anyway, Nick is a total idiot. Flemming is more like Martin.

'Hey,' Flemming calls across the room to Alyce, 'nice job.' See? Alyce Fuller just climbed one step closer to the top of the school ladder. She got twenty-five kids out of science for at least ten minutes. All she has to do now is pretend that she did it on purpose and she'll be on her way to personally addressed party invitations. Of course people would think she's a whole lot cooler if she'd stop saying 'Oh dear' every five seconds.

'Oh dear.'

'Alyce, relax.' Anyone would think she'd blown up the school. 'It's just a little smoke.'

'Gracie Faltrain, to the principal's office,' the loudspeaker breaks through the noise of the room. Okay, now it's time to panic.

'He sees a little smoke and it's, "Gracie Faltrain to the office".'

'What do you think it's about?' Alyce asks.

I shrug my shoulders. There are a million reasons why I could be called to the principal's office. And none of them are good.

Annabelle shoots me a smile that can only mean two things: she knows something and I am dead.

I run through the list of possible offences on my way down the corridor. I knocked over Fred Cazaar last week, but that was a complete accident. There was the small detail of being late back from lunch four times in a row, but the soccer field is a long way from the classrooms.

'Mr Yoosta?' I say, looking through the already open door. There's this policy in the school that the principal's office is always available to students. If you're listening from the corridor, you can pretty much hear whatever's going on inside. A lot of kids don't like it, but take it from someone who has spent her fair share of time in trouble, it's a good thing. It means he hardly ever yells and there's lots of room for a fast, easy getaway.

'Gracie, come in and sit down.'

'Okay. But if this is about Fred Cazaar, even he said it was an accident.'

'I'm sure it was, but this isn't about that.' He writes something on the paper in front of him and I make a mental note to keep my mouth shut from now on. 'It's about the Firsts. You must know you've caused a stir, a girl playing on an all-boys' team. You're quite a player.'

'Thanks, Mr Yoosta.'

He nods. 'You've earned the praise, Gracie, that's why this news is so hard to give you.'

'What news?'

'The coach needs my permission before he can hold tryouts for the Firsts. I have given it to him, on the condition that you do not participate.'

'What?'

'I know that this seems unfair, but it has been called to my attention that there are rules that must be followed. It is clearly stated in the Firsts guidelines that the teams are single-sexed.'

His words are emptying out of his mouth and onto the desk, spreading out before me like pieces of a puzzle I can't put together.

'I played in the National Championships; no one cared about that.'

'Yes. But those games weren't quite as rough, not like these. Gracie, that rule is there for a good reason. The organisers don't want to risk your safety.'

'But that's not their decision to make. I can take care of myself on the field. You've seen me. I belong in that team, Mr Yoosta.'

'Even if I agreed, there's nothing I can do. The Inter-school Sports Board would have to waive the rule.'

'So make them waive it.'

'Gracie, I can't. Their decision is final, and it has been made.'

I'm so angry that I can't speak, which is lucky because if I could, I'd tell Yoosta where to shove his Inter-school Sports Board.

I push my chair back and stand up. When I get to the door he calls my name again. 'Gracie, I am sorry. Coach has told me how hard you've worked. I've spoken to him about starting a girls' team. We think you would make an excellent captain.'

I ignore his comment. 'You said I'd been called to your attention. Who by?'

'The other teams,' he says, and his voice sinks soft as a pillow.

I don't need your sympathy, I think. I've proved I can cut it against boys. I've been proving it for the last five years.

I thump my fist against every locker on the way down the corridor, slamming the ones that are open. I imagine every second one is Yoosta's face. Every other locker is Annabelle. No prizes for guessing who asked the other teams to protest. Annabelle Orion knows practically every boy in Melbourne. She's dating the boy who hates me the most.

The bell goes as I walk back into the science lab, and I follow Annabelle out into the corridor. I let the swarm of kids protect me. Perfect. A million witnesses, all too busy pushing towards their lockers to see a thing.

'You think you've won?' I lean in close. Her breath smells sweet. Everything about her is a lie.

'Get away from me, are you crazy?'

To everyone else she seems innocent. Her eyes look like a lake that's cold and deep on a hot day. I see through her, though. Those eyes are shallow and lined with rocks. A person could break their neck believing in eyes like those.

'Who did you get to call the school, Annabelle?'

She shakes her head and looks around at the crowd gathering. 'I don't know what you mean.'

I draw my fist back ready to launch. I take a minute to enjoy the look of fear on her face. I take a minute to imagine the crunch of her nose, crisp as breakfast cereal at first, then soggy.

'I've waited eleven years for this, Annabelle,' I say, and then I swing, my whole weight behind it.

'And you're just gonna have to wait a bit longer.' Flemming catches my fist and picks me up. He pushes his way through the crowd and carries me, still swinging, down the corridor.

He walks across the schoolyard with Alyce running behind us. He doesn't put me down till he sees Martin coming out of the Year 12 block. I give him a sharp push once I'm on solid ground.

'Your girlfriend was about to smack Annabelle Orion in the face,' he says.

'Faltrain, we talked about this.'

'Martin, she got the other teams to call the principal, I know it. I'm not allowed to try out for the Firsts. Yoosta says that if I'm good I can captain the new girls' team.'

'You always wanted to be a captain,' Martin answers.

My blood feels like metal, my arms and legs and hands are hard with it, and the only way to feel right again is to hit or kick or yell. 'You don't think I can cut it in the Firsts?'

'Those guys play hard, Faltrain,' he answers.

'But I'm better than all of them, and you know it. We played them in the off-season games already.'

'That's different. Those games are for fun. These are rough. Scouts come to watch them. Those guys won't be doing anyone any favours.'

'You think I need favours, Martin? You think I only scored goals over the summer because everyone on the field let me?' I feel like my boyfriend has gone and some, some *guy* has stepped into his place. 'You're the one who needs favours, stuck in goal while Maiden takes your position. You didn't even try to get it back.'

'This isn't about me,' he says, and grabs my arm. 'Listen. I know you're good. I know that better than anyone.'

I snatch my arm back and keep walking. The Martin who wouldn't play without me at the Championships is lost.

'Gracie,' he shouts.

That's when it's clear I'm on my own. Martin has called me by my first name exactly once before today. I was Gracie walking onto that field in Year 7 and Faltrain on the way out. I earned it. Seems like I'll have to earn it all over again. I'm good enough, and I'll prove it at the tryouts.

I cut the grass with angry strides. This is what you get when you have a goldfish for a boyfriend. All of a sudden Martin has forgotten how many goals I've kicked, how many times I've won the game for us, how I'm the one on the field and he's the one in the goal square because he's too scared to get out on the field and fight.

'I thought I might try out for the girls' team, Gracie,' Annabelle says as I walk past. 'Martin said I'd be great.' I know she's lying, but her voice has a way of getting under my skin. My arms and legs go from solid metal to rust in record time. And then they crumble. There's nothing left to hold me together.

The rest of the day moves slowly. Martin doesn't say sorry. Flemming can't look me in the face at training. None of the team can. I want to be home, away from everyone who thinks I'm not good enough to cut it in the Firsts.

'It's not fair, Gracie. We'll do something about it,' Alyce says while we stand at the gates of the railway crossing. The lights start flashing.

'This gate is always blocking my way. Let's jump over. We've got time before the train comes.'

Alyce puts her hand on my arm. 'Be patient.'

'I don't want to be patient.' I flick words at her like stones. 'I want things to be the way I want them to be. Right now.' Patience might be all right for people like you, Alyce, but not for me. 'Martin doesn't think I'm good enough.' I kick hard at the peeling white paint on the wood of the gate.

'He's worried about you.'

'If he was really worried, if he really cared, he'd listen.' The train is so loud I have to shout to be heard. 'He wouldn't want me playing on a team with Annabelle Orion.'

'I know how you feel, Gracie, but . . .'

I cut her off. 'How would you know that? You've never tried out for anything in your life.' There's no way Alyce can get this. She has no idea what it's like to want something this bad and have it taken away.

The express rushes through the station. Once it passes I can see everyone still standing on the platform.

'There are other ways of being kept off the team,' Alyce says quietly as our bus arrives on the other side of the gate and takes off before we can cross.

'We've missed it.'

'There'll be others, Gracie.'

Don't you get it, Alyce? There won't be that one. That one's gone.

8

We have to let her play, Helen. If you
spend your life sleeping without
dreaming, what's the point?
Bill Faltrain

Dreaming's no fun in a coma, Bill.
You think about that.
Helen Faltrain

'Jane called this afternoon,' Mum says when I walk into the kitchen. 'She wants you to call her back.'

'Later, Mum. We've got an emergency on our hands. I'm not allowed to play in the Firsts because I'm a girl. You have to ring the principal. We have to take it to the High Court. It's discrimination.'

Mum wipes her hands slowly on the tea towel before turning around. 'Did the principal give a reason why he doesn't want you in this competition?'

'He says it's too dangerous, that the guys who play in the Firsts are too rough.'

'Maybe he's right, Gracie, love. I'm not sure I want you playing if you're going to get hurt,' Dad says with the same voice Martin used at school today.

'I can handle it. I've played in the National Championships – a *national* competition. I can play soccer against some Year 12 boys.'

'I'm siding with your dad on this one, Gracie. You can

captain the girls' team. That could be a great challenge for you.'

It takes me about two seconds to work out what's wrong with Mum's sentence. 'I never told you about the girls' team. The principal called you, didn't he?'

I feel like I'm in one of those movies where the hero loses everyone around her and she has to fight alone. 'I'm meant to be able to trust you and you're lying to me.' If they want a fight, I'll give it to them. All of them. 'You can't stop me, either of you.'

'Gracie Faltrain, don't take that tone with me.'

I know what's coming up. She'll say, 'I'm your mother. I clean up after you. I drive you to games.'

'I'm your mother.'

Here she goes.

'I pay for your medical expenses.'

Ouch. That was nasty.

'I'm the one who will have to look after you for the rest of my life if those boys give you permanent brain damage.'

Very, very nasty.

'And if I say the Firsts is too dangerous, then you won't play.'

She's talking without stopping to take breath. I'm starting to get an idea how she and Dad decided to get married. 'I am your girlfriend, Bill Faltrain. I go out with you. I kiss you goodnight. You will marry me.' Well, I'm not Dad, and she can't push me around.

'Mum, I'm in Year 11 and you don't get to decide everything I do.'

'I know how old you are, Gracie Faltrain, I gave birth to you.' Oh no. She's using the pregnancy defence. I have to do everything she says because she gave me life.

Except I don't. Not this time. Not when the thing I've always dreamed about is close enough to touch. There's only one answer to the pregnancy defence and everybody knows it. It's like using an atomic bomb to end a war, though; years and years of fallout follow.

'I wish you hadn't.' There's a slow whistle in the room as my missile locks on to my target.

'Now, let's talk about this.' Dad's voice is drowned out under the explosion. We both ignore him.

'Just because you're too scared to do anything, Mum, doesn't mean I am.'

'Go to your room,' she says, and I can hear the hurt in her voice. There's only one thing a person can do that's worse than the pregnancy defence. They can use inside information to their own advantage. I've just thrown what Mum told me the other night right back in her face. But everything's fair in love and war. Everything is fair in soccer.

'We only want to protect you, baby,' Dad says later, sitting on the end of my bed.

'I don't need protecting.' I keep my voice sharp, hoping it will cut through his blindness and make him see. 'The principal's brainwashed you. It's me, remember. My middle name is soccer.'

'And here's me thinking it was Elizabeth,' he says, and laughs.

'Dad, I need to do this. I need you and Mum to believe in me. Don't you get that?' I wait a minute. 'I believe in you.' When he asked me to trust that he wouldn't leave again I did. People can't get where they want to go unless the important ones around them go too.

'This is different. You could get hurt.'

'I'm so sick of everyone being too scared to take chances. Dad, it's my dream to play soccer.'

I've got him now. There's more than one way to get knocked down in life and he knows it. When he came back last year, he and Mum asked me if they could change the nursery into 'The Bookshop Plant Stop Café'.

'It's what we've always wanted to do, baby,' Dad said. 'But you have to agree, because it's going to take a lot of work, and we might need you to help us out sometimes.'

'It might mean money's tight again,' Mum explained. 'Is that okay with you?'

'I can handle that,' I'd said. I could handle anything if it meant having the two of them back together.

'I'll speak to your mum about the Firsts,' Dad says tonight. 'I'm not promising anything. You know she has the final word.' He rocks me gently and it feels like we're bobbing in a dark ocean.

I creep to my door after Mum and Dad think I've gone to sleep. They're in the kitchen talking.

'I don't want her playing, Bill.'

'Helen, you've watched her on that field. She comes alive out there.'

'It's not the alive part I'm worried about. It's the dead part, when those apes flatten her. She's not supergirl.'

'You can't keep her in cotton wool forever.'

Mum snorts loudly. 'Cotton wool? I've watched that girl fly too close to the sun all her life. She'll get burnt, Bill. And then what?'

'She'll rise again.'

'You live in books. This is real. This is mud and dirt and

boys who will think nothing of running right over the top of Gracie.'

'Helen, I know this is real. It's life. That's why you have to let her make her own mistakes. You have to let her live.'

'You weren't here last year when she was living, Bill. You didn't drag her out of bed because she wanted to hide from the world.'

'I know. But I'll be here this time, to pick her up if she needs me, like I'm here with you, every day in the shop, making things work. For us.'

Mum's quiet. I can't see her, but I know she's waving her hands around like long branches on a windy day. She always does that when she's worried. And Dad will be reaching out, making her quiet. 'Storm and stillness, Gracie, baby,' he'd said to me once. 'Your mum and I match.'

'Why do I have to let her live?' she asks after a while.

'Because, Helen, we both know what happens when you stop doing that.'

Mum puts a plate full of eggs and toast in front of me in the morning. 'Eat it all,' she says. 'You'll need the strength if you're going to try out for the Firsts.' She looks at me, her eyes holding mine. 'Your father thinks we need to support you in your dreams. His exact words.'

'What do you think?'

'I think some dreams get you killed. But I know better than to stand in your way.'

'So you'll talk to the principal?'

'Yes, and as of now you're relieved of duties at the shop. We're making enough money to hire someone else and you'll need all your spare time to study and train.' I kiss her hard on the cheek.

'I worry for you so much. You kick your way through life without seeing how dangerous it can be.'

'Danger's part of the fun, Mum.'

'Gracie, do you remember one summer, when you were in Year 4 at school? You and Jane wanted to sleep outside in your dad's tent.'

'We heard noises in the back yard.'

'You two were scared out of your minds, and you still wouldn't come inside. Too stubborn, the pair of you.' Mum shakes her head at the memory. 'Jane was so white in the morning from lack of sleep I was embarrassed to take her home.'

'But we were fine.'

'I know,' she says, and touches my hair. 'But I can't bear to see you scared, Gracie. You're my daughter. I guess what I'm saying is, play if you have to; just don't be too proud to come inside.'

'I won't. I'll be okay.'

I never told Mum, and neither did Jane, but I wasn't afraid that night. I knew the shadows on the wall of the tent were trees, not monsters, not 'psychotic maniacs, Faltrain', like Jane kept whispering. She begged to go in the house, but Jane hardly ever got scared, so I wouldn't let her. I knew she'd be disappointed if she did.

'See,' I said when the sun came up the next morning. 'We were fine.'

'Next sleepover, Faltrain, we stay in my house, in front of the TV, like normal people do.' She stuffed her sleeping bag into its cover with little punches.

'That wouldn't have been half as much fun, though, Jane,' I said.

The fun in life is the adventure. The fun is in taking chances.

9

Great boyfriend, great soccer, great life?
What a load of crap.
Gracie Faltrain

'Gracie, didn't your mum give you the message?' Jane asks when she calls before school.

'I didn't have time to call back. There's a lot going on here. Yoosta's been trying to keep me off the Firsts team. So has Martin. But we're making an appointment to see Yoosta later on today. One meeting with Mum and he'll be on our side.'

'That's great.'

'I know. It means I have to train hard. The tryout games are in just over a week. That's not a long time to get ready.'

'What's Martin's story, then? Why's he trying to keep you off the team?'

'He says he wants to protect me. He's gutless, Jane. I don't even want to speak to him anymore. The only thing I'm saying to him is, "I told you so", after the tryouts. Until then, I'm planning on ignoring him.'

'Don't you have a match tomorrow?'

'Don't need to speak to play.'

'I guess not. But Faltrain, Martin is your friend.'

'He's not acting like it. Why are you on his side?'

'I'm not on his side.'

And we're back to where we were in our last phone call. There's a note in Jane's voice that I haven't heard before. I'm not sure if she's mad at me, or if she can't think of anything else to say. In best friend land, both are deadly.

I'm saved by the doorbell. 'That'll be Alyce, Jane. I have to go.'

'Sure, Faltrain – well, good luck with the whole Firsts thing,' she says, and hangs up.

'Who was that?' Alyce asks.

She looks at her watch after I tell her. 'It's eleven-thirty at night over there. Is anything wrong?'

'Not everyone goes to bed at seven, Alyce.'

Nothing's wrong with Jane, unless you count that after eleven years of friendship we might finally have run out of things to say. I push Alyce out the door. Some thoughts are too awful to stand still for. If you do they'll sink into your skin and make you think about them all day.

'So is it true, Gracie?' Annabelle asks, walking up to Alyce and me at lunchtime. 'I heard you and Martin broke up.'

Suddenly lunch doesn't seem so appealing. 'You heard wrong.'

'It came from a reliable source.'

'Oh yeah, and who was that, Susan's writing on the toilet door?'

'Martin, actually.'

'You're a liar.' Martin might be acting like an idiot lately, but the last person he would talk to about me is Annabelle Orion.

'He told me he's sick of being with a girl who thinks she's a boy.'

'Whatever you reckon,' I say, but even as I do, I can feel the day folding in on me like a letter. Annabelle is about to lick the envelope and post me to Siberia.

I've known her as long as I can remember. I've seen her lie to teachers about me. I've seen her lie to the whole school about me. Her eyes get greener; greedy, like she has stolen a whole chocolate cake and needs to eat it quickly before someone takes it back. She talks slowly today, lets her dessert sit on the plate.

'He said that you're always out to prove something – he reckons you do it to show your dad how good you are, to make sure he sticks around.' It's the last two words that convince me. They're straight out of Martin's mouth.

Annabelle knows she's won. She smiles, puts me through the mail slot and lets the metal flap clang shut. From inside the box I can hear her slowly licking each finger, finishing her cake.

It's not that I believe her about Martin and me breaking up. He knows if he did that without telling me first it'd be him getting broken. It's that he gave Annabelle a part of me. The biggest part.

You'll be sorry, Annabelle. Everyone will. Mum will beat the Sports Board and then I'll beat everyone trying out for the Firsts. The bad guys never win. Everyone knows that.

Everyone except the bad guys, that is.

Mum is yelling so loud when I get home I can hear her from the street. I haven't seen her mad like this since they stopped showing the old movies on Sunday afternoons. 'There were two coaches from the other teams there. One of them told me that I should control my daughter, Bill. Control her. As if she were a dog that needed a leash.'

'Perhaps you should relax, Helen,' Dad says. Looking at Mum today, there's no way even Dad will be able to calm her down. It's like he's facing a tornado with a kite strapped to his back.

'He said the other schools felt it would be ridiculous to have a girl playing in an all-boys' competition. I said the only ridiculous thing was that sort of attitude in the twenty-first century.'

Dad starts laughing.

'What?' Mum snaps.

'I was remembering another time I saw you this angry.'

There's a time for strolls down memory lane, Dad, and this is definitely not one of them. We're having a crisis.

'You'd seen me with my sister and thought I was on a date,' Dad says.

'She looked so surprised when I tipped that drink over your head.'

'She liked you right from the start,' he chuckles.

Mum doesn't even seem angry anymore. My dream of the Firsts is starting to look like a car wreck on the side of the road.

'Guys, focus,' I say, walking into the lounge room. 'I'm still not allowed to try out. We still have a problem.'

'It's not polite to listen at doors, Gracie Faltrain,' Mum says. 'No, at the moment they have not changed their minds. But you have earned the right to be on that field. And you will be on that field.'

It seems pretty clear to me tonight, though, that there's no way I'm playing in that competition. If Yoosta faced Hurricane

Helen and it didn't change his mind, I can't imagine anything that will.

'It doesn't look like parental intervention will help,' Alyce says when I ring her.

'What? All I know is that if Mum can't help, I'm stuffed.'

'I'm sorry, Gracie.'

'Sorry won't change things. Everyone thinks that the girls' team is where I belong. It'll help my leadership skills, Yoosta said. I know where I'd like him to shove his leadership skills. Right up his . . .'

'Gracie,' Alyce cuts me off. 'I have to go.'

'What?' The single biggest catastrophe of my life and she has to go? How about saying she'll be over in five minutes to watch TV and eat as many blocks of chocolate as it takes to make me feel better? 'Alyce, I thought you could come over and watch a DVD.'

'I can't tonight. Maybe after the game tomorrow?'

What could she possibly have to do that's more important than helping me? The rules of friendship clearly state it has to be something big: a death in the family, a fire in the home.

'I've got homework.'

Homework? 'It's not even a school night.' Alyce Fuller, you are not normal. I hold on to the phone for a few seconds after she hangs up, listening to the long beeps echoing in my ear like a flat-line signal from *ER*. Gracie Faltrain, welcome to the end of your life.

I email Jane and spend the next half an hour staring at my inbox waiting for an answer. I guess she's not available either. Great boyfriend, great soccer, great friends, great life? What a load of crap.

10

They're muscles.
Declan Corelli

Yeah, right. Muscles. Spelt b.o.o.b.s.
Gracie Faltrain

There's nothing more disappointing than an empty inbox. Welcome Gracie Faltrain. You have no messages. Nada. Zero. Zip. Zilch. I can't believe Jane didn't write back. What, she's so busy in England that she doesn't have time for me anymore? I eat breakfast slowly, filling up that small hope that she'll call before I have to leave.

Usually soccer takes my mind off everything; even the thought of playing is enough. Not today, though. It's in my head that this won't be my team for long and it's ruining the day like rain.

'Hey, Faltrain,' Corelli calls out to me on my way up to the field. 'Can we talk?'

I follow him round the side of the change rooms. 'What?'

'I wanted to ask. My brothers are home from uni for the weekend.' His words are going all over the place like his kicks.

'What is it, Corelli?'

'They'll be watching me.'

'So?'

'Pass me the ball?'

I can't stop thinking that he has the chance to try out for the Firsts and I don't. What makes Corelli good enough to play and not me? Some testosterone? No boobs? I have more testosterone than Corelli. And he has more boobs.

'If you want the ball, take it,' I say. Corelli shouldn't get a place just because he's a boy. I'm better than him. I'm better than all of them. And I can't afford to feel pity for anyone if I'm going to prove it. I need the old Gracie Faltrain.

'Sorry, didn't realise you were trying out for soccer girl of the year,' Corelli says. He acts tough, but I can see the hurt carving up his face.

'Come on, now. You know you're the only one on this team with a real chance at that title.'

'You can't drive life in reverse, Gracie,' Dad said when he moved back home after the National Championships. 'So make sure you're happy with the direction you're going.'

Clearly I have a different model of car from his, because warming up today, I feel like my wheels are spinning backwards at high speed. Martin tries to catch my eye but I ignore him. He doesn't come over to talk. Lucky for him. It's hard to be goalie with both your kneecaps smashed in. So everyone in the school thinks I can't cut it in the Firsts? Well watch this.

I let Flemming have the ball for a minute and then I run in and take it. Just like old times. I can't afford to look at the faces of my team; I focus on the ball. My legs are faster than everyone on the field. I scoot past Singh, Francavilla and Maiden. I arrive at the goal with time to spare. No one's on my back. I take the shot. Goal one: Gracie Faltrain.

'What's the matter with you?' Flemming asks on my way past. I ignore him. I'm my own team again. I run at the ball.

I swerve around the opposition's defence and then past Corelli, who's standing there like an idiot. It's not my problem his brothers are watching. I fly in and score goal number two.

'Faltrain,' Martin says at half time. 'Don't do this.'

'Do what?'

'You know what. Stop playing like you're alone out there.'

'I am alone, Martin. That's the point.' I turn away and wait for the whistle to start me again.

I'm ten minutes into the next half when I make my mistake. I look up. And in the background I see Corelli's entire family, pressed against the wire fence, watching. He's standing like Alyce at a party, all on his own with nothing to do.

He's close enough to take the goal and far enough away for him to be a hero if he makes it. His eyes are small round dots, two tiny sprinkles alone on a huge cake. 'All right, all right.' I kick the ball in his direction. It lands so close even Alyce couldn't miss it. I ghost along beside him, blocking anyone who gets in his way. I didn't give him the ball so he could stuff up.

Corelli runs in close to the goal square, lines the ball up perfectly, and takes the shot. He's jumping around with his shirt over his head like he's kicked the winning goal in the World Cup. 'He looks like a complete idiot,' Flemming says, but he's smiling.

'At least now we know where he gets it from,' I say. 'Listen to that.'

'Go Corelli, woo hoo!' echoes from the crowd.

'And that's his mother,' I laugh. 'Ten bucks says she does the Mexican Wave on his second goal.'

'You're on.'

When play starts again I move towards the ball and line up

another shot for him. I'm ruined. I can't play for myself anymore. And soon I won't be able to play with the team, either.

Corelli kicks two goals. The whistle goes. His family does a sort of dance. 'Pay up, Flemming.'

'No way. That's not a Mexican Wave. What is that, Corelli?'

He's too busy dancing himself to answer. Singh rubs my hair. 'Thought for a second the old Faltrain was back.' Francavilla picks me up and shouts like a crazy man. I feel shut out the whole time, though, because I know I won't be there when they win in the Firsts. I'll be watching from the side. It's not the team's fault, but I can't stand to be with them just the same. It hurts too much to be around what I can't have.

Jane still hasn't emailed me when I get home. It's the first time I haven't spoken to her after a game. 'It's not over till it's over, Faltrain,' she'd say if she were here. I pick up a piece of chocolate and sandwich it between two chips. 'Oh it's over, Jane. Believe me, it's over.'

11

The world's brutal. And if you're not
the sort of person who can leap into it
head on then you're the sort of person
who gets squashed in the rush.
Gracie Faltrain

'You'd think they'd want to know how I'm doing,' I say over breakfast on Monday morning. 'Neither of them has called all weekend. Alyce didn't even come to the game. I could be dead, for all they know.'

'You're not dead,' Mum says. 'And some people do have lives that don't revolve around you . . .'

Ouch. Lucky for me the phone rings and cuts Mum off. She looks like she has a whole lot more to say.

'Hi,' Alyce says when I answer. She acts as if she hasn't done anything wrong.

'I'm sorry, who's speaking?'

'Gracie, I just rang to say I'll meet you at school today. I've got some homework to do in the library.'

'What homework is more important than me?' I ask after I hang up.

'More importantly, what homework haven't you done that Alyce is doing?' Mum answers.

'None.'

'Don't "None" me. Get to school and find out. I'll keep fighting, but you need to stay out of trouble.'

Alyce is sitting at one of the computers when I walk into the library. 'What homework did we have?'

'You know – that assignment for English. You already handed it in.'

'I did?'

'Stop worrying about schoolwork and start thinking about the tryouts.'

'No point in doing that. I'm ready enough for the girls' team.'

'Gracie, there's nothing wrong with a girls' soccer team.'

Maybe that's why Alyce has been ignoring me. She's mad. 'I never said a girls' team wouldn't be good. It's just, it won't be my team. I won't be playing with Martin and Flemming and Francavilla, the guys I started with.'

'I said stop worrying. I have a feeling that everything will work out fine.'

That's easy for Alyce to say. I'm not like her. I can't sit back and wait and hope that I'll get what I want. That's why she was alone until we became friends. It's why she'll never get Flemming without my help. It's why no one likes her. That sounds harsh, I know, but the world is harsh.

Last night on the news they showed this riot that erupted at a football game. The crowd started pushing and all these people were trampled. Dad saw the look on my face and flicked the channel.

He doesn't get it. I see stuff like that every day. I see Annabelle Orion walking over the top of Alyce because she's too little to matter. I see myself, sitting on the sidelines of the most important competition of my life, because I'm a girl.

'I'm not like you, Alyce. I can't sit back and wait for things to be okay.'

'Gracie, you're yelling. People are looking at us.'

'Have some backbone, Alyce. Who cares if people are staring?'

She turns around to her computer and keeps typing. Typical. No wonder Flemming doesn't know she's alive. Being good gets you where Alyce is. Waiting gets you where Dad is. It gets you nowhere. If I can't play in the Firsts then at least I'm going out with some dignity. I'll show every boy in that competition that I'm good enough to beat them, that the only reason I'm not playing is because they're too scared to go up against me.

I slam the door of the library. The wood bounces against the frame. I feel better than I have in days.

'Annabelle,' I say when I get to her locker. 'Tell Woodbury to meet me in the park next to the school at five o'clock tonight.'

'And why would I do that?'

'Because if you don't, I'll tell everyone that I challenged him to a kick-off and he didn't turn up. You wouldn't want your boyfriend's mates thinking he's scared of a girl, would you?'

'Dan's not scared of you.'

'Then there shouldn't be a problem.'

'Faltrain,' Martin calls as I'm walking to class. 'Wait up.'

'Get lost, Martin.'

'We need to talk.'

'About what? How you told Annabelle I'm scared my dad'll leave again?'

'Is that why you're still mad at me?'

'I'm mad because you're an idiot. Annabelle is the reason I can't try out for the Firsts and you're talking to her like she hasn't done anything wrong.'

'Faltrain, I'm sorry. I should've kept my mouth shut. But I thought if Annabelle knew about your family, she'd understand why soccer's so important to you. I thought maybe she'd call her friends off. But she's only one of the reasons Yoosta won't let you play. It's in the rules that the competition is strictly boys only.'

'You don't think of me as a girl when I'm on the team.'

He laughs and scratches at his arm. 'I pretty much think of you as a girl all the time, now, Faltrain. Those guys are fierce. I don't want you to get hammered every match you play.'

'I won't, Martin. When I'm out on that field I don't feel like a boy or a girl. I don't think about that at all. I think about winning and taking the shot. I think about soccer.'

He keeps scratching at his arm. 'I know. Flemming knows too. He feels bad that he let you down. The whole team does. We all saw what you did for Corelli. So, we decided: either you try out, or none of us do.'

In my whole life I've only heard three things that have made me so happy I could cry. Dad telling me he's coming home. Martin telling me I'm the one. And this.

'What?' Coach roars at practice after school. The whole team has turned out to support me and it feels great. We're all standing in front of him except for Corelli, who's standing with his testosterone, ready to run, near the door. 'What are you telling me, Knight?'

'That if Faltrain doesn't try out, then neither do we.'

'I don't have a team without you.' Coach is moving from angry to desperate. Any minute he's going to cry.

'Exactly,' Martin answers.

'I've tried already,' he says, sitting down and sighing. 'Faltrain, I've been in there at least three times, and every time he tells me the same thing. The Inter-school Sports Board has to waive the rule. And they won't.'

'Then we don't enter a team,' Flemming says. 'Simple.'

Everyone leaves one by one after that, feet dragging across the ground. Martin and Flemming and I stay. I have that same feeling I get when I lose a game. Except this time it's worse. I've lost the entire season in one day.

'So I should let the Board know we're out?' Coach says, his eyes drifting upwards, like a kid who has lost his balloon. Martin and Flemming look at me. I find myself looking for that balloon, right along with Coach. There's only one right answer. I want so bad to give the wrong one, but I start to shake my head.

'Wait . . .' And then there's a tiny knock on the door. 'Alyce?'

'Hi,' she says shyly, so soft the wind outside almost steals it. She doesn't look at me directly, just passes two pieces of paper over. As soon as I read them I want to hug her so hard she squeaks. But I can't get close enough. My angry words from this morning are still sitting between us.

'So that's what you've been up to.'

'I didn't want to tell you until I was sure it would help.'

'What is it?' Martin asks. 'Hand it over, Faltrain.' He takes the paper from me and starts to laugh. 'Has Yoosta seen these?'

'I gave copies to him this afternoon,' Alyce answers. 'He's read my email to the paper explaining what's happening to

Gracie and their reply to say that they are very interested in writing a story about it. Seems it's a topical issue.'

'Have you heard back from him?' I ask.

'That's what I came to tell you. He called me into his office after the last lesson. He contacted the Board. He says this could convince them to let you on the team. This isn't the sort of publicity they need or want when the finals, and some of the matches, are being televised and reported in the local papers.'

'Does that mean I'm in?'

'I don't know, Gracie. But I think you should get your mum to make another appointment with him. Get her to bring your dad too, and tell her to take this.' Alyce hands me another letter. This one's from the paper to Mum and Dad, explaining that they're very interested in writing my story.

'But Mum didn't write to the paper.'

'I know that,' Alyce says, and smiles. 'But no one else does.' Like I've always said, there's more to Alyce than meets the eye. A whole lot more.

As we walk outside Flemming's smile is bigger than anyone's. 'Alyce saves the day,' he says, kicking the ball hard and chasing after it.

That's the first time he's said her name, so I'm betting that blush on her face goes all the way down to her toes.

'We should celebrate,' Martin says. 'What do you want to do, Faltrain?'

I look at my watch. Four forty-five. 'I'd like to buy Alyce a doughnut. I just have to do one small thing on the way.'

'One small thing, huh?' Martin says, looking at the crowd of kids standing in the park. 'There must be fifty people here.'

I recognise some of the guys from the off-season games. They seem taller, though. I guess guys can grow a lot in a few months.

'What are they waiting for?' Flemming asks.

'I'll take a lucky guess and say – Faltrain,' Martin answers. He turns to me. 'What did you do?'

'I challenged Woodbury to a kick-off.'

Martin stares at the crowd. 'Good plan.'

'It seemed like it was at the time.'

'You want some help out there?' he asks.

'Nope. This is something I have to do alone.'

As I move, the crowd closes in like a fist with fifty fingers. 'Actually,' I look back at Martin and Flemming and Alyce. 'Maybe you could just make sure that this *is* something I do alone.'

The four of us walk out into the middle of the crowd. This isn't exactly how I imagined it. 'Life never is, Faltrain,' Jane would say. I know she's right, but just once, I wish that things would turn out as I picture them in my head. And I'd like this to be that one time.

'See you invited some friends along, Woodbury,' I say when I reach him.

'I can't help it if there are a lot of people who want to see you beaten, Faltrain.'

'It's a shame they're going to be disappointed.'

'How do you want to do this?' he asks.

'We play a twenty-minute game. Just you and me against each other. The one who scores the most wins.'

'Who are the goalies?' he asks.

'You pick yours. I'll pick mine.'

'Fair enough,' he says, walking over to the crowd and talking to a guy at least twice my size. Martin starts moving towards the goal.

'Good luck, Gracie,' Alyce says.

'Thanks. And Alyce, I'm sorry I yelled at you today.'

She shrugs. 'We can talk about it later, Gracie. Now, get out there and use your anger in a good way.' She sounds like one of those videos they make us watch in Personal Development classes and Flemming starts laughing next to her.

'Good luck, Faltrain,' he says. 'Although something tells me it's Woodbury who's gonna need it.'

The light is dropping by the time we start. It's hard to see. Shadows of birds cartwheel across the sky. The crowd casts dark shapes. Woodbury and I stand opposite each other. The ball sits on the ground between us. 'When the whistle goes,' he says, 'it's whoever kicks first.'

It seems like hours before someone blows the whistle. I keep my body tense, ready to jump. I take a quick look at Woodbury. He's standing the same way. We've both got everything to lose. And everything to gain.

The sound hits the air and my legs move a second too late. Usually I'm quicker than light, quicker than breath at the kick-off, but today my nerves are sand in my blood.

Woodbury has feathers in his, hundreds of them. He races down the field, feet cradling the ball. I'm too far behind to stop him. He swings to the right before goal and kicks. The smack of his boot is hidden in cheers.

But it's my old friend in the square today, confident, unafraid. Martin dives left and catches the ball. Score nil. If I keep playing like this, though, it won't be for long.

I shake my arms and wait for Martin to throw the ball back onto the field. He sends it as far as he can in my direction. Woodbury and I chase it. I get there first and kick it forwards. I'm a second ahead – less, half a second – but it gives me the edge. I slam the ball and hope it's hard enough to take the goalie by surprise. He slaps it like a summer fly, lazy with heat.

'Good try, for a girl,' someone calls out from the crowd.

If I lose today, I won't be the player who wasn't good enough. I'll be the girl who wasn't good enough. Woodbury's goalie tosses the ball in, and I follow it like my life depends on it. My soccer life does.

I have the edge, now. Because I'm more desperate than Woodbury. I go in hard. Over and over again. I've had to play like this all my life because on that field I have more to prove.

'Get under them, Faltrain, get around them,' Martin always said. So I do. I race around Woodbury, dancing with the ball in the dark afternoon. I crash it into the net, a wave of leather hitting the back like the shore.

'Go, Faltrain,' Flemming calls from the side. Alyce gives a little half squeal like she does at the matches when she gets excited.

'Lucky kick,' someone yells.

Lucky, hey? How's this for luck. I head the ball forwards after it's thrown in and race hard. Woodbury's close, but as always, not close enough. He doesn't have a chance. This is what I do. I run faster than anyone else. I kick goals. I remember once my dad said after a game, 'You play like a champion. But I have no idea how you do it.'

I knew what he meant. Why are some people good at things and others not? He and Mum aren't great at sport. Alyce is more like them than I am. But somewhere along the line I learnt to run. Somewhere I learnt to pass and kick and shoot. No one taught me. When I watched my first soccer game I knew. That field was home.

I can feel Woodbury give up beside me at about the sixteen-minute mark. He moves slower. His feet fumble at the ball. He can't catch up now and he knows it. I could ease up and still win, but I don't. I launch the ball like a boat; watch it sail across the sky. I keep slamming it into the net. I keep winning.

Someone blows the whistle. Flemming and Martin and Alyce run towards me. 'Guess there are a lot of disappointed people out there, Woodbury,' I say. 'And you must be one of them . . .'

Martin grabs my arm and pulls me away.

'I haven't finished talking yet,' I say, and then I notice the crowd moving in on us.

'Quit while you're ahead, Faltrain. One person you can win against. Fifty, I'm not so sure.'

'Loser,' Flemming says to Woodbury as we leave.

Martin walks Alyce and me home to my place. 'Why don't you call your parents and tell them you're staying for dinner?' I ask her. 'You want to stay too, Martin?'

He shakes his head.

'What's up? You've been quiet all the way home.'

'Geez, Faltrain. You hammered the guy in front of all his mates and you didn't even shake his hand.'

'You reckon he'd have shaken mine if he'd won?'

Martin shrugs. 'Forget it, then. See you tomorrow.' He waves goodbye to Alyce and walks off.

I should have known it was too good to be true. The old Martin might make an appearance every now and then, but he never stays around for long.

12

The important thing to remember
about lying? You're probably not the
only one who's doing it.
Jane Iranian

'So you're saying you want me to lie, Gracie Faltrain, is that it?' Mum asks as we sit down to dinner.

'Let's not think of it so much as lying as not telling the truth.'

'She's your daughter, Bill.'

'Well, you would have written to the paper if you'd thought of it,' Dad answers.

'Mum, if it makes you feel any better, you can write to them and wait for a reply, but do it tonight or it'll be too late.'

She slams my dinner down in front of me. Alyce jumps.

'Now that would be a waste of time, wouldn't it? Tell me again what it is you want me to say to the principal tomorrow.'

'Say we've spoken to the paper and they're prepared to write a story about how unfair this is, about the fact that until this year the school hasn't had a girls' soccer team and so I haven't had a choice. Tell Yoosta to tell that to the Board.' I read from Alyce's notes while she looks guilty beside me.

'Bill, I'm really not comfortable with this. Can't you talk to him?'

Whoahh there, Mum. I need a shark tomorrow, not a jellyfish. 'You're the one who spoke to him before; he already knows you,' I reason with her. 'I'm not asking you to outright lie. Just bluff a little.'

'You owe me after this. You owe me dishes every night and rubbish bins on Thursdays.'

'Anything you say, Mum.' Anything to have the chance to be in the game.

'Remember, winning is the most important thing.' I give Mum a pep talk before she walks into Yoosta's office after school. She gives me the look that says, 'You are no daughter of mine. You were dropped on my doorstep at night by strangers.'

I quit while I'm ahead. One thing I know about Mum: you don't want to push her too far. She's just as likely to turn around and do what she thinks is the right thing.

Dad, on the other hand, is plasticine in my hands. Actually, looking at him before he walks into the office, he's just plasticine. No good to me at all. He stands there twisting his fingers together and looking guilty. Mum's definitely my only hope.

Martin and I hang around in the corridor until Yoosta invites them into his office. After that we get as close to the door as we can.

'So, Mr Yoosta,' Mum says, 'we've written to the paper and they're very interested in the Inter-school Sports Board and their policy of discrimination against girls.'

'As I said to you before, Mrs Faltrain, I sympathise with Gracie. I have been at many of her matches, and she is a remarkably strong player.'

I elbow Martin in the ribs. 'Hear that?'

'However,' Yoosta keeps going, 'I do think it's an exaggeration to suggest that the Board has a policy designed to discriminate against girls.'

'The paper doesn't think it's an exaggeration,' Mum says.

'I have spoken to the Board and advised them that should Gracie be excluded from the competition, you will make this an issue in the media. Is that correct?'

'That is correct, Mr Yoosta.'

'That being the case, they have given me the authority to advise you that your daughter can play in the competition. They do not want that sort of publicity.'

'It's as easy as that?' I can hear suspicion thick as Corelli in her voice. Don't blow it, Mum.

'I did assure them that I would do everything in my power to dissuade you, Mr and Mrs Faltrain, but I can see where your daughter gets her determination from. I must say this, though. The competition is rough. There will be boys twice her size on that field.'

'Mr Yoosta, my daughter is one of the best players on that soccer team. She has trained with those boys since she was in Year 7. She has proved herself countless times, kicked countless goals and, although I'm not proud to admit it, kicked countless heads.'

Go Mum. Go.

'My daughter may do many stupid things . . .'

Don't go there, Mum, don't go there.

'But one thing I know for sure. I'd be more worried about the other players than her.'

Now would be the time to stop. Unless you want me playing on the prison soccer team.

'Very well,' Yoosta says as their chairs scrape on the floor. 'I just want you to be sure about this. Have you seen the Firsts play? I have to be honest with you; I believe Gracie will get hurt.'

His words make Mum hesitate. 'Thank you for your concern,' she says, 'but this is something that Gracie has to do.'

Martin's spinning me around in the corridor when they walk out. 'I take it you've heard, then,' Mum says. 'I don't want to know how.'

'You are legends.'

'Just prove him wrong, Gracie Faltrain. Just make sure you prove them all wrong.'

'Relax.' This is what I'm good at. This is what I was born to do.

'So what's your plan for the tryout match next week?' Flemming asks through a mouthful of chips.

'Same as always,' Martin answers for me. 'Steal the ball and kick the goal and kick anyone who gets in her way.'

'And if some guys play rough and slam into you?'

'They won't,' he jumps in again. 'She doesn't need a plan for that.'

'I'm just saying,' Flemming says, grabbing his jacket, 'it doesn't hurt to be prepared.'

'She's prepared.'

Ever feel like you're the only one who doesn't know what the conversation is really about? There are other ways of speaking, like kicking someone under the table, or wiggling your eyebrows up and down. Martin and Flemming are having a whole different conversation from the one I'm listening to.

'Something's up, Martin,' I say on the way home.

'What do you mean?'

'I mean there's something you're not telling me about the tryout match. Spit it out.'

'Faltrain, what happened last time I lied to you?'

'I let the air out of your bike tyres.'

'And?'

'And I gave you that tiny scar on your leg.'

'That tiny scar took four stitches.'

'I was aiming for the ball, not your ankle.'

'We weren't playing soccer.'

'I wasn't talking about that ball.'

'Look, Faltrain, forget about Flemming. He should be worrying about himself, anyway. He's still failing every subject there is to fail except for sport. You're not the only one who has problems,' he says, looking past me to his front steps. Mr Knight is sitting where he usually is these days, staring out at the street.

'How was practice?' he asks as Martin walks past him to go inside. Mr Knight always makes me feel like I've just lost a game, even though I tried really hard to win. Martin shrugs. 'Okay. You want a coffee?'

'Thanks, mate.'

I smile at him and then follow Martin inside. About a month after we won the Championships, Martin invited me round to his place for dinner. 'Your dad looks so sad,' I said to him as he walked me home afterwards.

'He's a hundred times better than he was before, Faltrain. He's moved from the couch to the front steps.'

If he's a hundred times better, Martin, then what's bothering you so much? If things are really going to improve you have to take a chance and find your mum. Martin doesn't take chances, though. He's like Alyce. What the two of them don't realise is that if you never take a risk you wind up sitting on your verandah, dreaming about a life that only exists in your head.

I listen to Mr Knight's mumbled thank you as Martin takes his coffee out to him. I hate the way everyone talks in this house. It's a made-up language that means nothing. The real stuff is being yelled underneath everyone's skin, way down in their blood. You keep all your yelling in your blood for long enough and it'll poison you.

Martin walks back into the kitchen and starts pulling meat from the freezer. He puts it in the microwave to defrost. He starts slicing into vegetables.

'Was it like this, before she left?' I ask.

'Like what?' He takes the meat and presses it onto the frying pan. I hide my answer under the spitting fat. 'Empty?'

He squashes the steak until it's flat and dry. 'I know you don't get it, but Dad's different since I came back from the Championships. You didn't know him before. He never even hugged Karen. He didn't have the energy. He asks about our days, now. Mum hasn't been here to do that since I was a kid.' He looks at me. 'So what does it matter what it was like before she left.'

I don't answer. Because it wasn't a question.

'Mum,' I say later in the evening while we're watching TV, 'what if you knew a way to make things better for someone, but they were too scared to let you. Would you still do it?'

'That depends on what you're really talking about, I guess.'

'I think maybe I know a way to find Martin's mum. Alyce

gave me the idea when she wrote in to the paper. I thought I could put an ad in or something.'

'No, Gracie Faltrain.' Her voice is a slap. 'You mind your own business.'

'But I want to help him.'

'Sometimes help can be the thing that breaks a person.'

'How?'

'Because it's the thing that gives them hope.'

'But hope's a good thing.'

'Only when there's a chance; other than that it's just bad news in disguise. Imagine that your father hadn't come back to us last year, and we'd had to find a way to make it through without him.'

'But he didn't do that. He loves us.'

'But imagine he did leave, and you spent every day wishing that he would come back – because you would, Gracie. Every soccer game you'd search for him. After a while, though, you'd have to stop hoping. If you didn't, you'd be stuck looking up into the stands for the rest of your life.'

'That's why I have to do something. Martin still thinks about his mum.'

'Of course he does. But he doesn't hope for her to come back, Gracie. You're the one who's doing that.'

'How can you be sure?'

'I've watched your team play for almost five seasons now. Martin nearly broke my heart in those first few years. Your father used to say he looked as though he was out at sea, searching the crowd for something to stop him drowning. He doesn't look into the stands for his mum anymore, Gracie. He looks at you. He trusts something again and it's taken him a long time to get there. Don't mess with that.'

Mum's wrong. Martin is still lost at sea; he's just so good at treading water these days it looks like he's swimming. And if I'm the only one who can see that then I have to do something. Because that storm is coming, and if all I do is wave at Martin from the shore, he'll drown. Friends don't sit on the sand and let that happen. Not real friends, anyway.

13

Love sucks. Just ask Romeo and Juliet.
Or me.
Jane Iranian

Jane's acting less and less like a real friend at the moment. It's been five days since I emailed and she still hasn't replied. She didn't call me after the game. I want to ring her and yell, 'Don't you care about me anymore?' And I would. But Gracie Faltrain knows a thing or two about dignity.

We're in stand-off mode. It's happened with other friends. You're close for ages, so close you could spin off the secrets from their diary like a Frisbee. Then gradually, one of you disappears into the distance like a bad throw. They only call twice a week. And then once. And then not at all.

I never thought that would happen with Jane. If you'd asked me a month ago I would have told you it was impossible. I'd have bet my life on it. I know everything about her. She wears pyjamas with little bears on them. When she was a kid she was scared of the dark and had to sleep with her bunny lamp on. I know she liked Matty Fletcher in Year 4 and punched him in the face when no one was looking because he didn't like her. You just don't give someone that sort of information on yourself and then walk away.

I stare at the phone. Ring. Ring. Ring.

'What are you doing, Gracie?' Mum asks.

Testing the strength of my telepathic powers over long distances to make my best friend need me again. 'Nothing,' I answer, and pack my bag ready for school.

The only way out of stand-off mode is for the person who's walking away to realise what they're missing. I have to give Jane some time to be Gracie Faltrainless. She'll see what she's missing. She'll come running back.

In the meantime, I have Alyce. 'Come inside for a minute,' I say when she arrives. 'I want to try to straighten your hair.'

'Gracie, I sort of like my hair the way it is.'

'But don't you want to love it?'

'Well . . .'

'Exactly. Now sit tight for a minute.' Or sixty. Or a hundred. Alyce could solve the world's energy problems with the static electricity coming from her head.

'Does it look any better?' she asks after about fifteen minutes. Better than what? Better than if you'd stuck your finger in a power point? 'It definitely looks shinier.'

'You know, technically it's not shinier because it's straighter. It's just that the light reflects off it more easily now that there's a flat surface.'

'Alyce, one day your brain is going to explode,' I say, and push her out the door.

'You look really pretty,' I whisper at the start of class. 'Flemming will love it.'

'Keep your voice down. I told you, I don't like him.'

'Right. You don't like him. You love him.'

'Shhh, Gracie.'

I'm too busy teasing her to notice what's going on around me. Big mistake. School is a dangerous place for people like Alyce. I should have known to keep an eye out for enemies, especially enemy number one: Annabelle Orion. It's the end of period two by the time I realise she's been listening to us. And by then it's way too late to do anything about it.

Alyce and I are sitting next to Flemming in English. We've teamed up to work on poetry. Every group gets a different topic and together we have to write a poem and read it to the class. 'Remember, it doesn't have to rhyme,' Mrs Wilson says. 'The best poems are the ones that surprise the reader.' That's her story now. My poems are always surprising; she never says she likes them.

'So,' I whisper to Alyce when Flemming's at the front getting our topic. 'I heard he's failing school.'

'Who?'

'Flemming. Martin says Yoosta wants to kick him out unless he starts getting better marks, so I thought you could offer to tutor him.'

'What? No.'

'It'd be the perfect chance for you to spend some time together.'

'I said, no. Leave things alone. Please.'

Flemming walks back to our desks. 'We got jibbed. Wilson gave us nature. Why couldn't we get something like soccer or surfing? Who writes poetry about frigging nature?'

'A lot of people, actually. Wordsworth and Keats,' Alyce says.

Oh no. Don't let him know you like poetry. What, are you running for nerd of the year?

'There are some really beautiful lines in them,' she says.

'Can we copy them?'

'That's cheating,' she answers.

I kick her under the table. He's joking, Alyce. Laugh. But she doesn't. She picks up her pen and looks as serious as if she were a doctor about to operate. 'Okay, first line?'

Flemming and I start flicking through our books, looking everywhere but at her pen.

'We could do one about the soccer field – that's nature,' Alyce says. 'What's the ground like before you run on it?'

'I dunno. It's sort of flat and new. And . . . green,' he answers.

'You idiot,' I say.

But Alyce writes it down. 'It's good.'

'I'm a poet and I know it,' Flemming says with this look on his face like he's just won the smartest guy in the school award and Alyce is the one who's given it to him.

'You're a loser,' I tell him.

But he keeps on going, giving Alyce lines about soccer and she keeps writing them down. She changes a few, but mainly it's exactly as Flemming tells it to her. He loves it. He loves it so much he volunteers to read it out to the class.

He changes colour about five times when the teacher raves about how good it is. 'I wrote it,' he says. I could not have scripted the whole thing better. Who could have known it would be this easy? I'm so excited I forget the first rule of life: nothing is ever easy.

Annabelle Orion is the last to read her poem. She walks past and gives us that smile that I know all too well. I saw it on her face when she told our kindergarten teacher that I pushed her off the swings. I didn't. Annabelle Orion fell all on her own, but she wasn't about to miss an opportunity to land someone in trouble and steal a bit of attention. She framed me with the skill of an expert criminal at the age of four. That smile means one of two things: we're dead. Or we're about to wish we were.

She stands at the front of the class and waits a minute to make absolutely sure everyone is listening. 'Our topic is love,' she says, and I have a flashback to period one. I'm using my big, fat, stupid mouth to tease Alyce about Flemming. And Annabelle is sitting behind us.

I have to hand it to her. Annabelle covers herself beautifully. There is no mention of Alyce Fuller. There is no mention of Andrew Flemming. But when she finishes reading her poem there's not one kid in the room who does not know who Annabelle is talking about. The school nerd is in love with the school soccer star. Either Alyce is hot for me or Flemming, and either way it's not good for her.

I watch Flemming watch Alyce raise her hand. 'May I please be excused?' she whispers. 'I don't feel well.' Her cheeks are two circles of tomato soup, hot enough to burn. Mrs Wilson lets her go. The whole class sniggers as she walks out the door.

Flemming doesn't say anything. He just got the first A of his whole school career because of Alyce and he sits there and lets her take the heat. Idiot.

I throw my pen at Annabelle after she sits down. 'I will get you,' I mouth across at her and draw my finger along my throat.

As soon as the bell goes I run. There are only two places a girl will go when faced with humiliation of that level. First to the toilet, to cry her eyes out. And then when she feels a bit better, to the tuckshop, for some serious comfort food. Alyce is still in her crying stage.

I knock softly on every door.

'Go away,' a little voice echoes across the tiles.

'Alyce, come out or I'm coming under.' The door clicks and swings open. She looks like she's been swimming in the ocean with her eyes stretched wide.

'I've been worried about you.'

'Why? Because every kid in the class knows I like Andrew Flemming? I'm never leaving here, Gracie.'

'Your parents'll eventually notice you're missing.'

'I don't care.'

'Alyce, Annabelle will pay for this.' I grip her shoulder, so she can feel how strong I am. 'We'll make her pay.'

'Gracie, I've told you a million times. I don't want to make Annabelle pay. I want to be left alone.' She washes her face and leaves without another word.

No way, Alyce. I'm not letting you disappear again. Your days of losing are over. Whatever I have to do to shut Annabelle Orion up for good, I'll do it. And that's a promise.

14

Alyce Fuller smiles at me as she's
walking up to her seat. Man, that chick
has killer eyes.
Brett Mason

To win anything at all, though, you have to risk something. Unless Alyce can do that, she'll always lose. She'll never leave where she is. It's not enough to stand on the platform and wish for the opportunity train if you're not ready to get on when it pulls into the station.

She's in the crowd with Mum and Dad this Saturday, watching our last match before the Firsts competition starts. There's a group of kids sitting about ten steps down, closer to where the action will be. Not Annabelle's crowd. Kids like Brett Mason, the kind of guy who'd let you into the tuckshop line if you told him you were in a hurry. But in a million years Brett would never ask Alyce to sit with them. He wouldn't think of it. Because people like Annabelle have told people like Brett that Alyce currency can't buy anything at school.

I've watched her get carried around in people's wallets for a while. In Year 6 Alyce hung out with Francesca Ring. In Year 8 she sat with Hailey Nelson. By Year 9 she was on her own most of the time. She was just too different. Until she met me.

I'm not passing her on. I'm increasing her market value. Pretty soon everyone in the school will wish they'd held on to those Alyce shares. They could have bought their mum and dad that snazzy house by the beach they'd always wanted.

If fate brought Alyce to me, then it's because I can make things different for her. She's like those mice I saw on the Discovery Channel last week. The scientists were exposing them to UV rays to test how quickly they developed skin cancer. Mum had to leave the room. Dad and I watched right to the end. I wanted to see what happened to those little guys, trapped in wire cages, sunning it up. Nothing happened, though, because mice's bodies are smart. The more you expose them to something they don't like, the more they change to shut it out. Those mice were growing little thirty-plus coats over their skin to block out the rays. They'd have to bake for hours before the scientists could see a difference.

Alyce has only been in the sun with me for six months. She just needs more exposure. I'm not saying I want her to get so popular she fries. I'd be happy if she had a tiny tan.

Alyce acts as if she doesn't care. I can see her chatting away to Dad like she always does before the game, her hands shaping some character out of air for him to see. Don't encourage her, Dad, I think. Alyce has to live in this world. The real one.

'What are you thinking about, Faltrain?' Martin asks, stretching next to me.

'Alyce.'

His eyes trail along the stands till he finds her. 'She loves talking to your old man.'

'She needs to hang out with people her own age. Where does talking to Dad get her?'

'It gets her happy, Faltrain.'

'It won't make her fit.'

'Alyce fits fine. It's everyone else who's wrong.'

'Majority rules, Martin. You ever hear of that?'

'You sure you don't want Alyce to change so your best friend isn't the biggest nerd in Year 11? I know you miss Jane.'

'That's not it, Martin. Anyway, Freddy Jabusi is the biggest nerd in Year 11. Alyce is at least second on the list.'

I change the subject. Talking about Jane makes me feel sick. If she doesn't call tonight it will make two matches that she has missed.

'So how much do you think we'll win by today?'

He shrugs. 'Just play your best, Faltrain, that's all you can do.'

'Don't you care if we win?'

The old Martin cared, the one who pulled me aside during my first game and told me how I could make it.

'You care enough for both of us,' he says, and walks off to goal.

I don't get it. If he feels like that, why not quit soccer altogether? What's the point in being on the field if you're not planning on winning?

I fight fierce today. I make sure we win. Look at me, Alyce and Martin, see what it feels like to take what you want. I stare up into the stands at half time and see Alyce, huddled under a blanket with Mum and Dad. Martin looks cold, too. I'm hot, heart pumping the heat up under my skin to at least forty degrees.

Martin and Alyce keep piling on the layers like those little mice. I guess they figure that way they'll never have to face up to anything. That won't work, though. Underneath all those layers, they're still Alyce and Martin, even if no one else can see.

15

Touch Faltrain and I'll touch your face.
Martin Knight

'Right. Listen up,' Coach yells on Tuesday afternoon. 'If you're not here to try out for the Firsts, then you're in the wrong place.' He laughs for a bit at his own joke. No one else does. This isn't funny. This is serious. This is it.

'I want two practice matches, short ones, to give me an idea of how you play. After those I'll make my decision. List'll be up in a few days.' He waves his hand down the middle of us and then divides each group again. He calls out the positions. He gives me my usual one. From his wink I'm pretty sure it's not an accident.

Martin's on the other team as goalie. Flemming's playing with him. Singh's with me, but other than that, everyone else on my team is new. Coach blows the whistle and we're off.

Jason Newman collects me on the way past and knocks me flat. And he's on my team. No prizes for guessing this is going to be a rough game. It won't do any good to complain, though. I have to prove I can win against guys like Newman. If I can't, then there's no way Coach will pick me.

The ball's kicked towards centre and I run. 'Arms down, Hakka,' Coach shouts, but it's too late. Callum Hakka cracks me with his elbow and I hit the ground. Again. The thing about that opportunity train I was talking about? It's not only important to be on it, you have to make sure you're not under it, either.

At the end of the first half Coach calls me over. 'It's getting rough out there. You want to come off and play in the next match with Francavilla and Corelli?'

'No.' I say it as hard as the ground felt when I smacked against it. Harder. If Coach pulls me out now, then everyone will know I can't cut it. 'Don't worry about me. Worry about them.'

'Get a drink, then. You've got five minutes.'

I look around for Martin but he's not with his team. He runs back on late. 'Watch out, Faltrain!' he calls as Newman trips me. I get a face full of dirt and an ear full of Jason's laughter. He's about to get a game full of Gracie Faltrain.

'You're meant to be on my team,' I yell. But since you've rewritten the rules, let's see how you like them.

I run at Jason. Fast. I take the ball. There's no time to play games. I head straight for the goal and shoot. Martin doesn't do me any favours. He wants to get on the team too. He dives for the ball and misses by a hair. A beautiful, thin as silk, hair. Goal number one: Gracie Faltrain. Soccer isn't about being a boy or girl, you idiots. It's about skill. It's about sending the ball home.

I'm too fast for them this half. I'm too good. I chase the ball into the corner near our goal. I'm on an impossible angle, but there's no one near to send it to. I'll have to mail it myself then. I flick the ball up so I can shoot with my right leg. I kick it as hard as I can. Goal number two. I'm in. I can feel it.

'I did it, Martin,' I laugh as we lie on the edge of the field, watching the second match.

‘Never doubted you for a second.’

‘Really?’

‘You’re a hundred times better than anyone else out there, Faltrain,’ he says, and my bones tingle like they do when he kisses me. Before I can thank him Annabelle walks up and stands over us, blocking the sun.

‘You want something?’ I ask.

‘I just came over to congratulate Martin.’

I can feel anger making my arms and legs twitch. Who does she think she is, congratulating my boyfriend? ‘Get lost, Annabelle.’

‘You think you’re better than everyone else just because you’re on the soccer team. You only scored goals today because at half time Martin and Andrew threatened to bash anyone who touched you. Face it, Gracie; you’re out of your league.’

‘You’re just jealous,’ I start, but then I see Martin’s face, covered with guilt. I wait until Annabelle has walked away.

‘You rigged the match? You said I was better than all of them.’

‘You are. But you haven’t played against guys desperate to get a place. It’s rough. They’d decided to knock you to the ground. We evened the score.’

‘But the score’s not even when it comes to me, Martin. Don’t you get it? I’m not like everyone else. I’m a girl, so I have to be better. I have to be able to do it on my own, all of it, or it’s no good.’ He’s quiet. ‘But that’s it, isn’t it, Martin? You really don’t think I can.’

‘I think you’re a better soccer player than all of us put together.’

‘So why rig the tryouts?’

'Because . . .'

'Say it, Martin.'

'I don't know if it'll be enough.'

I can duck all the insults that Annabelle has to throw at me, but that one sentence from Martin hits me full in the face.

'Stop trying to make me like you.'

'And what am I like, Faltrain?'

'You're scared all the time. You weren't like that last year.'

'You should be more scared. Those guys are going to play rough and you need to be ready for it.'

'I don't want to live like you,' I say, and run home. Maybe if I'm fast enough, I can get away from his words before they take hold.

'Gracie, baby.' Dad holds on tight to me tonight as I cry. 'I've seen you out there. You're better than any of them.'

'Martin rigged the tryouts.'

'Did he put the ball on the end of your boot? Did he have a remote control steering it towards goal?'

'No.'

'Seems like all he did was make sure they played fair.'

'I want the old Martin back, the one who told me to have guts and get the ball.'

'Martin cares about you, Gracie. He wants to protect you.'

'I've told you before. He's the one who needs protecting.' I explain my storm theory to Dad.

'The eye of the cyclone.' He nods. 'It's the scariest part.'

'But if he'd face his mum, things would be better, I know they would.'

'I'm not so sure, Gracie. You know how cyclones and hurricanes start?'

'No.'

'They get their energy from water that's as warm as the sun on your skin. And they don't stop until they hit colder oceans. You force Martin out of the only good memories of his mum that he has into the cold reality, and it might hurt him more. Are you willing to risk that?'

'Taking risks is what life's all about, Dad.'

'It's what *your* life is all about, baby,' he says. 'Think about that.'

Thinking doesn't save people, Dad. Sometimes you have to act.

16

I told you that love sucks. But is
anyone listening to me? No.
Is anyone calling to check on me? No.
England could fall off the map and you'd
all just smile and keep playing soccer.
Jane Iranian

Life shouldn't be hard.

'If it wasn't like that, though,' Dad said last night before he turned off my light, 'how would anyone really learn anything?' And then he left me lying in the dark.

What a load of crap, Dad. Why do people have to learn the hard way? Why did I have to find out from Annabelle that my boyfriend doesn't think I can cut it on the soccer field anymore? Why does Alyce have to hang around half her life waiting for Flemming to wake up and smell the roses?

I'm sick of life being hard. If Flemming won't smell the roses himself, then I'm going to grab his face and shove it in them. Next, I'm going to fix things for me. I'm going to train so hard that I show everyone what real soccer is. I'm going to be faster and better than I was before. I'm going to show Martin that living like a coward is wrong – as soon as I start talking to him again, that is. And I'm taking Jane back. A quick phone call's not beneath my dignity. I'll make the conversation short and sweet, show her what she's missing.

I wake up early to ring her.

'Faltrain, hi, I . . .'

'This has to be quick, Jane,' I cut her off. 'I only have five dollars left on my phone card until next month.' I don't want her thinking I'm desperate. 'I need some advice about how to set Flemming and Alyce up.'

'Like I told you before,' Jane says after I explain the situation. 'Think before you do anything. Take your time and use a bit of tact.'

'Look at all the great lovers they make us study in school. Romeo and Juliet. That guy Othello,' I say. 'They didn't take their time.'

'Yeah, and what happened?'

'I don't know. I never bothered reading them.'

'They died, Faltrain.'

'Oh. Well that's depressing.'

'I think that's probably what Juliet said when she woke up next to a dead Romeo.'

'You're just like Martin. Would it hurt to be a bit more positive? I'm trying to do a good thing for Alyce here.'

'I just think it wouldn't hurt to be a bit more sensitive. You don't want people laughing at Alyce. It's awful when you don't want to go to school because the whole place is making fun of you. There's this girl over here who was set up on a date and the guy didn't really like her –'

'Yeah, but this is different, Jane. Flemming likes Alyce, I know it.'

'Look, you asked for my advice, Faltrain, and that's what I'm giving. Be careful with Alyce. I have to go now. It's late over here. Mum's yelling at me to hang up.'

'I didn't hear anything. What's wrong? You're being weird

lately. You're not acting like my friend at all.'

'I'm not acting like your friend?'

'No. There's stuff going on in my life and you don't even care. You didn't ring after the game. I emailed you, no reply . . .'

'Faltrain, you ever think that maybe there's stuff going on in my life other than you?'

'I guess you have heaps of new friends over there, no time for the little people.' I wait for her to tell me something different. I want her to say, 'Faltrain, stop being such an idiot. You're the only best friend I need.'

There's silence on the line. And not a puddle of it either. I'm talking silence the size of the Indian Ocean. A person could drown in silence that big.

'Jane?'

'That's my mum calling again. I have to go,' she says, hanging up.

Be careful with Alyce? Since when does Jane Iranian give advice like be careful? When I first tried out for soccer, most people told me that playing on a boys' team was too dangerous. 'Ignore everyone, Faltrain. Being careful isn't living. Being alive means getting out there, getting knocked around.'

The Jane I know wouldn't tell Alyce to be scared all her life. She'd say, 'Get out there and break some bones; at least then you'll feel something.' That's got to be better than putting yourself on ice, making sure you're numb.

'Gracie? Are you okay?' Mum asks.

'Yeah. Why?'

'You're talking to the toaster.'

'Jane and I just had a fight. We never fight.'

'I can remember a few times you two disagreed.'

'Like when?'

'Like the time Jane's cousin came to stay in Year 7 and you were so angry that she wasn't spending as much time with you as before. Jane invited you along to everything but it wasn't good enough.'

'They kept talking about things I couldn't join in with, family holidays and stuff.' I wish Mum hadn't reminded me of that. I'd forgotten what it felt like to have Jane push me away.

'It feels like she's not interested in what I'm doing anymore. She's missed calling me after two games.'

'Gracie, the only way to find out is to ask. Maybe you're both changing, I don't know. One thing I am sure of – if you ask her, Jane is the sort of person to tell you straight.'

That's exactly why I won't be asking, Mum. I want to keep her for a little bit longer.

Jane's right about one thing: a little sensitivity with Alyce and Flemming is probably the right way to go.

'So, I heard you're failing school, Flemming,' I say at lunch.

'Who said I'm failing?' he asks, putting his sandwich back down on the plastic.

'Everyone's saying it.'

'Who's everyone?'

'Kids, Coach.'

'Coach?'

'I heard him telling Martin that he'll be needing a new centre forward if things keep going the way they are.' I feel bad lying to Flemming, but the end justifies the means, right? And this end will help Alyce.

'From the way he was talking, I'd reckon your dad might get a phone call tonight.'

'Another one?' Flemming asks, putting his head in his hands. 'My dad's gonna kill me. He lost it completely when the year level coordinator called last week. He said I'm off the team if I don't catch up.'

Hang on. Forget love. There's something much more important at stake. With Martin in goal, Flemming's the second best player we have on the field. We need him to win.

'So do the assignments.'

He doesn't answer. 'Flemming? Flemming?' I push his name at him.

'I can't do the stupid homework, all right.' His voice sounds like mine did last year after the guys kicked me off the team. I had nothing without soccer. Flemming looks like he's missing a layer of skin. Everything burns when you're like that. Everything hurts.

'Soccer's the only thing I'm good at, Faltrain.'

I don't bother telling him anything different. He and I are too alike for lies. 'So I'll help you.'

'Yeah, right. You're almost as bad as me at school.'

Okay, some lying is good. 'I meant I could get Alyce to help you.'

'No way.'

'What, you didn't actually believe Annabelle, did you?'

'It's not that.' He bites his lip so hard I feel it. 'She'll think I'm dumb.'

'Alyce doesn't care about stuff like that. She's friends with me, remember?'

'I guess you're right.'

'You don't have to agree so quickly.'

He doesn't laugh, just keeps looking down. Flemming shouldn't be like this. He belongs on the soccer field, fighting his way to goal. He's inside out, now. People shouldn't let their tags show to the world. It's not right.

'There are about twenty assignments overdue,' he says.

'Twenty?'

'You reckon she'll mind?'

'No way.'

I lean casually against the bricks until he's out of sight. And then I bolt. I need to find Alyce before she finds him.

She's in the library, as usual. I can't quite read the look on her face when I give her my news. It's a combination of horror, happiness and confusion. There's a fair amount of fear in there as well. I guess when you think about it, love's a mixture of all four. I remember when I thought about kissing Nick last year I felt like I had a volcano bubbling under my skin. 'Get too close to a volcano, Faltrain, and it'll burn till you're ash,' Jane would say if she was here. Her voice doesn't sound like it usually does in my head. Up until a few weeks ago, it was strong and clear, as if she was standing right next to me. Today her voice is an echo.

'So, you're okay with helping him? Alyce? Hello, anyone home?'

'Gracie, I can't,' she whispers.

'Why not?' I whisper back, even though I'm not sure why we're being so quiet. No one's here except for us. 'It's twenty assignments. You could do them in your sleep.'

'You heard what Annabelle said in class. Imagine what she'll do when she knows I'm tutoring him.'

'Who cares what Annabelle Orion says about you? It's perfect. Flemming needs help. You get to save the day. It could be the script for a film.'

'Right. Next you'll be telling me that with a little makeup

and new clothes Andrew will come right out and ask me to the dance.'

'There are lots of films where the nerd gets the guy, Alyce.'

'I think you're meant to tell me I'm not a nerd.'

'Alyce, close your eyes and relax,' I say. 'Stop being so scared for a second.' Coach has us do something like this in his pep talks. It's about seeing who you really are, not who you are when you're afraid.

'When you think about spending all that time with Flemming, what do you really feel? Think with your heart and not your head. What does it tell you?'

She closes her eyes for about half a minute.

'Well?' She blinks.

'Alyce?'

'It tells me not to hope, Gracie.'

I was really hoping she'd say it told her to be excited.

I guess that's one of the big differences between Alyce and me. The first thing I do is hope. I hope so hard when I see that the final list for the Firsts has gone up, my head almost explodes. If I'm not picked, I'll never prove that I could have made it on my own.

'So look who's on the team.' Annabelle drags her finger down the paper and hits my name. 'With her boyfriend's help, that is.'

I turn to Alyce to roll my eyes but she's gone. That's the way it is, now. When Annabelle Orion's around, Alyce Fuller isn't, like smoke on a windy day. I run my eye over the rest of the names. Flemming is there, for now. So is Martin. Most of our guys made it, too.

'Everyone in the other Firsts teams is laughing at you,' Annabelle says. 'They're saying that there's no way a girl could cut it in the competition.'

'Is that what your boyfriend's saying? I cut it against him last week.'

'Let's see. The last thing he said about you was that he'd like to see you dead.'

Ouch.

'He says that if you play in the competition, then they'll treat you like all the other guys. He gives you five minutes before you're out of the game. No one's doing you any favours next Saturday.'

'She won't need favours, Annabelle,' Martin says, standing next to me. Too little, too late, I think, and try not to notice that he's wearing the blue jumper I like so much, the one that makes him look as hot as summer. Cool it, Faltrain. No amount of sexy jumpers makes up for what he did.

'I don't need help.' I look at Martin. 'From anybody.' He walks away without a word. Annabelle trails after him.

'She's my punishment, you know,' I say when Alyce miraculously blows back into town.

'Don't be stupid, Gracie,' she answers, straightening her glasses. 'No one has done anything bad enough to deserve that.' I watch Annabelle flirting with Martin at the drinking taps. And I have to agree.

'So the Firsts games start next Saturday,' Coach says on Friday afternoon. 'There's no game for you tomorrow, so make the most of the relaxation. Next week we're up against the best team of the competition.'

'Stop worrying,' Flemming says. 'We thrashed them in the off-season games.'

'I'll stop worrying when you start,' Coach barks. 'You think this is going to be easy? You think that and we're finished before we even get out on the field. Give me five laps. And that means everyone.'

'Good one, Flemming,' I say, my heart screaming in my chest. 'Just remember to do one thing before you open your mouth next time.'

'What's that?'

'Shut up.' I overtake him. I need to finish these laps so there's time to die before the rest of practice.

'All right,' Coach yells when we've finished. 'Listen up. We've got four new players. Wrecker, King, Marsters and Cheng, welcome to the team. You'll play with Dalton as our strikers. Don't stuff up. These are the other positions. Knight, you're still captain and goalie. Francavilla, Bennett, Singh, Buckley and Morieson, you're in defence. Faltrain, Corelli and Maiden, you're in midfield. Flemming, you're centre forward. Now get into pairs. I want to see some solid kicking.'

Martin grabs hold of my arm. 'You're still mad, aren't you?'

'What makes you think that?'

'You're about to ask Corelli to be your tackle partner. I never give you the silent treatment after you've annoyed me, Faltrain, think about that.' And then he turns around and smacks straight into Corelli. I put my hand out to help my new partner up. I leave Martin lying on the ground.

'Can't we talk?' he asks again after practice.

'Get lost,' I say. 'Happy? Now we've talked.' I grab my bike and cycle home. Just because he's a goldfish doesn't mean that I am. I wish I was, though. I wish I could forget that Martin thinks I'm not strong enough to make it.

***

‘Flemming?’ I say when he picks up the phone.

‘Yeah?’

‘It’s Faltrain. I forgot to give you Alyce’s number at practice.’ I read it out to him.

‘You left pretty quick,’ he answers.

‘I had stuff to do.’

‘Me too. I told Dad I’m getting a tutor and he said I can play in the Firsts, if I hand in all my overdue assignments. I have to come home every night, though, and do work.’

‘That sucks.’

‘You’re telling me. Knight and Annabelle were going to the movies after practice and I have to come home and write about some stupid guy who kills his wife because he’s jealous.’

Hold the phone. Hold anything. ‘He went to the movies with who after training?’

‘Annabelle.’ Flemming’s voice turns as soft and flaky as fish.

‘When did they organise to go to the movies?’

‘Look, maybe this is something you need to talk to Knight about. I don’t know the whole story.’

‘So now there’s a story about the two of them? Since when do they have a story?’

‘Faltrain, you need to calm down.’

‘I have to go, Flemming.’

‘You’re not going to do anything stupid are you?’

‘Just worry about your homework.’ Let me worry about Martin and Annabelle.

‘I’m going out to see a film, Dad,’ I say as soon as I’ve hung up. ‘I really need you to drive me.’

I don’t talk on the way. I watch the lights racing past us and let them blur together. Martin is mine, Annabelle. Mine with a capital M.

'Are you all right, baby?' Dad asks before I get out.

'I'm fine.'

'Do you need to be picked up?'

'Martin will be taking me home. I'll be back by nine.' This won't take long.

I slam the door and walk towards the café where I know they'll be waiting until the film starts. I catch sight of them before they see me: Martin and Annabelle sitting alone together. I've never felt so sick in all my life. First she takes Nick, then she tries to take soccer. She's not taking Martin.

I walk up to the table. 'Faltrain, what are you doing here?' Martin looks more than surprised. He looks scared.

'I think the question is: what are you doing here?'

'Seeing a film . . .'

'Do you want to come too, Gracie?' Annabelle asks.

I lean in as close as I can to her face. 'Get lost, Orion.'

'Faltrain, what's wrong with you?' Martin asks, pulling me away from her.

'I think we all know the answer to that question,' Annabelle says.

'Don't you have somewhere else to be?' I ask, clenching my fist.

'Can you give us a minute?' Martin asks her, and she walks off in the direction of the toilets.

'Coward,' I say to him after she's gone. 'You can't even tell me to my face.'

'Tell you what?' His voice is a kite floating above us, high and tangled.

'You're cheating on me with Annabelle Orion.'

'Are you crazy?'

'Flemming told me everything.'

‘I don’t know what he told you, because there’s nothing to tell. Anyway you’re the one acting like you want to break up.’

‘When I want to break up I’ll tell you. Annabelle’s a cow, Martin. She’s only here to get back at me.’

‘Not everything is about you, Faltrain. If you weren’t such a cow we could have gone to the movies together.’

‘I was a cow for a good reason. Annabelle’s a cow for no reason. There’s a huge difference. And anyway, I’m here now. So tell her to get lost.’ My voice is cardboard, crunching in my mouth.

‘You can come with us, but I’m not telling her to go.’

Annabelle walks back and sits down. ‘So, are you coming, Gracie?’ If I leave now then she’s won. Don’t smile too soon, though, Orion. You’re ahead in the first half. But it’s nowhere near the end of the game.

Martin sits between us, his elbows squashed close to his chest. Annabelle offers him chips and he takes a huge handful. Stop feeding my boyfriend, I want to yell. He doesn’t even like salt and vinegar chips. He likes chicken. I’m in the middle of my worst nightmare and I can’t wake up.

‘You don’t even like that flavour,’ I hiss at him before the film starts. ‘You like chicken.’ I shove the packet I’m holding into his face.

He takes another handful from her. ‘Thanks, Annabelle.’

He’s loving this, I think. I lean over and snatch her chip packet. I empty every last one over his stupid, grinning head. ‘How do you like them now?’ I yell, and leave before the film even starts.

It’s Mum who answers the phone when I ring. ‘Slow down. I can’t understand you. You’re where? On the corner of what? I’ll be ten minutes.’ I have to hand it to her; she knows how to respond to an emergency call. Take the details and drive. Ask questions later. She's at the corner in eight minutes. Record time.

'Dad said he took you to meet Martin. Do you want to talk about what happened?' She takes her eyes off the road and looks at me for a second. 'You're as white as a ghost.'

A ghost is what I'll be on Monday morning, when everyone finds out what's happened. Martin doesn't belong to me anymore. It'll be like seeing Annabelle arrive at school wearing my lucky soccer shirt, bragging about how many goals she kicked. Has the whole world gone crazy? I can actually feel my eyes about to launch themselves out of my brain with all the pressure that's building up.

'Right, Gracie Faltrain,' she says, pulling over to the side of the road. 'Talk.'

'He was there with Annabelle Orion.'

'And you think that means he's breaking up with you?'

'He was eating salt and vinegar chips. From her packet.'

We pull back out onto the road. 'Did you ask him why he was there? Maybe they're just friends.'

'He can't be friends with her and me.'

'You can't own people. You can't make them do what you want them to.'

I twist the ring Martin gave me around and around on my finger.

'Gracie? Do you trust Martin?'

'He fixed the tryouts and lied to me. He was at the movies with Annabelle.'

'He fixed the tryouts to protect you,' Mum says, turning the car in the wrong direction. We drive along a road that's mostly dark, dotted with tiny reflectors to mark the way.

'Where are we going?'

She swings into a car park. 'Falconer Lake.'

'I never even knew this was here. How come it's so close to our place and you've never taken me before?'

'We have. When you were a kid. You know, last year at the Championships, I saw the way Martin looked at you, and my stomach fell about twenty floors. I knew he meant business.'

'He's changed since then. He doesn't even play soccer like he used to. He just stands in the goal square, watching.'

'And you think that makes him a coward?'

'Maybe.'

'You think that I'm a coward, too, I guess, for going slowly with your father. That's what you meant the other day, in our fight about your soccer.'

The car feels smaller all of a sudden. The engine's on and the heater's running. I could write on the windows with Mum's breath. I shrug. 'You explained already. You're fixing things.'

'We are. A little every day. Gracie, I remember we went to a huge barbeque at this lake one weekend. Everyone else was already here when we arrived. All the kids were playing at the edges of the water. I was still getting things out of the car and you just took off. Your dad chased you, but he was too slow.

'You ran up to a rock at the edge of the river and water-bombed in. We thought you'd broken your neck for sure and then you bobbed to the surface like a cork, waving and calling your dad a chicken because he wouldn't go in. You were so disappointed with the day, because none of the other kids would jump. Everyone at that barbeque thought you were crazy.'

'Thanks, Mum. I'm glad we had this little chat.'

'The point is, not everyone wants to risk their neck. Doing things differently doesn't make you a coward. It makes a person who they are. Let Martin explain about Annabelle.'

'He won't talk to me. I emptied a packet of chips on his head.'

'I expect he'll get over that.' She starts to back out of the car park. 'You've done worse. Trust Martin to tell you the truth. And then trust your own judgement enough to believe it.'

That's good advice, I think as we pull into our driveway. The light from the back porch casts a faint glow over us as we walk towards the door. It was dark for most of last year, but Dad put a new globe in when he came home. Mum still walks slowly and carefully, even though she doesn't have to anymore. Because now we can see.

17

'Dump her, Martin,' Annabelle says after Faltrain leaves. I'm laughing too hard to answer. Faltrain's straight down the line, that's why I like her. Besides, if she was really angry, she'd have thrown her Coke as well.
Martin Knight

I'm up early this morning, ready to ride over to see Martin. He arrives at my house as I'm wheeling my bike onto the street.

'Going somewhere, Faltrain?'

'It can wait.' I lie my bike down on the nature strip and sit next to it. Martin drops down beside me.

'It was Mum's birthday yesterday,' he says eventually.

Perfect. It was his mum's birthday and I emptied a packet of chips over his head. Bad girlfriend. Or I guess bad ex-girlfriend.

'I just didn't want to go home last night. You left straight after practice and Annabelle was there . . . Things are getting better; Dad's trying. But some days I just don't want to go home, because I know he'll be there trying so hard it hurts him.'

'Martin, something happened to you at the end of last season, didn't it?'

'I had a fight with Dad, before I left. I told him how sick I was of everything – him, and Karen, and the house. I was so tired of him using us to lean on and giving nothing back. I walked in after the Championships and the house was sort of clean. Karen said he'd been out looking for work. He started trying.'

'You're allowed to want more than that, Martin. Let me help you find your mum. We could put an ad in the paper, see if she replies. You could ask her why she left.'

'No.' His voice is a sharp kick.

'Why not? You told me once that your dad spends his life looking backwards. What could be worse than that?'

'At least he's looking now. Before, he was staring into space, not seeing anything. Meeting her again – it'd kill him. I know it.'

'But what about you and Karen?'

'Faltrain, there's a difference between wishing Mum had never left and wishing she'd come back.' He looks past me to the house across the street and grinds his teeth. He's slowly scraping her out of him. Just like his dad did. 'Promise me you won't do anything.'

But if I do that, then I'm saying it's okay that you're only half as happy as you could be, Martin.

'Promise, Faltrain.'

'I promise.' I hug him with one arm. I keep the other shoved down deep in my pocket, fingers crossed tight. 'You can trust me.'

18

To win a little you have to risk something.
To win big you have to risk it all.
Gracie Faltrain

'My name is Martin Knight. I'm seventeen years old and I'm looking for my mother. Her name is Alison Knight and she is forty-five years old. She is also the mother of Karen Knight. If you're out there, Mum, I need to talk to you. Is that right?'

The man on the phone reads my advertisement back to me. Now is my last chance to pull out.

'That's right. I want to run it for two weeks. How much will that be?'

'Ninety dollars. How are you paying?'

'MasterCard. Helen Faltrain.'

I figure if you're lying, make it a big lie. I've got a month before the statement comes in the post. Live it up, Gracie Faltrain, I think. She'll ground you for a year. Even if I'm grounded it'll be worth it to save Martin.

I do remember that day Mum was talking about at Falconer Lake, parts of it at least. I leapt off the edge of that rock, and slammed myself at the water. It felt good to be freezing for a while and then warm inside a towel while I ate hot hamburgers.

And I remember all those other kids, paddling at the edges, who didn't know the half of it. To win a little you have to risk something. To win big you have to risk it all.

19

Hanging out with Fuller isn't as
bad as I thought. 'What do you do when
you're not reading?' I ask her.
'I work on cars,' she says. 'And sometimes
I read football magazines.'
'You making fun of me?' I ask.
You know, she's not bad looking
when she laughs.
Andrew Flemming

'Hi, Alyce?'

'Yes.'

'It's Andrew Flemming.'

'Oh. Hi. It's Alyce.'

'Yeah, you already said that. Look, Faltrain mentioned you might be able to tutor me.'

'Yes, of course. That would be fine.'

'Okay, then, so I'll see you after school. I can do half an hour in the library, before practice.'

'And that was the whole conversation?' I ask Alyce as we're getting changed for sport.

'Word for word. Was it okay?'

Sure. If you're a robot. 'Maybe next time change "that would be fine" for "great" or "fantastic". It's snappier. More fun.'

'I said the wrong thing.' Her face crumples. 'Boys never call me. How am I meant to know what to say?'

'You did great. Anyway, the important thing will be this afternoon. What are you planning on talking about?'

'His homework.'

'Wrong answer. You need to talk about other stuff. Show him you're interested in things besides school.'

'Like reading?'

'Maybe something you both have in common.'

Alyce and I are quiet. 'We don't have anything in common, do we?' she asks after a bit.

'I'll find out what he likes. And then you can lie,' I say as we walk towards the basketball court.

Alyce and I stand in line waiting for the captains to pick teams. The teacher chooses different ones today. And Alyce still gets called out last.

'Maybe you should tell Alyce to be herself with Flemming. Let him see her how we do,' Martin says when I ask him at lunch for the inside goss on Andrew.

Sure, Martin. And Santa Claus really comes down your chimney on Christmas Eve and leaves presents under the tree. I watched Alyce nearly kill herself scoring a goal today. For the opposite team. In a million years being herself will never work.

'Come on; give me something to go on. I'll do the rest.'

'Okay. He likes cars, soccer and football, and films about cars, soccer and football. He hates school.'

'Thanks, Martin.' I can work with that. So can Alyce. All she needs is a little imagination.

***

'But how can I talk to him about all that stuff if I don't know about it?' Alyce asks before she walks into the library after the final bell.

'Do what kids do every day at school,' I say. 'Make it up.'

'I don't want to lie about myself, Gracie.'

For someone who spends all her time reading, Alyce doesn't have a whole lot of imagination. 'It's not lying. You use most of the truth and mix it with about three-quarters of lies to make your life sound a bit more interesting.'

'What parts should I lie about?'

How can Alyce be so dumb and so smart at the same time? She has no idea how to survive at school. It's like in soccer: there are some plays you have to keep to yourself until the last minute. If I was Alyce, and I'd been born with an IQ that was rocketing up the charts like a bullet, I'd keep it under wraps. I'm not saying I wouldn't use it, but you wouldn't find me sitting up the front of the class advertising myself as Einstein. I'd hang back, slouch a bit, pretend I didn't care.

In all the years I've known Alyce, she has cared about everything. In Year 6 she ran a stall at the school fete to raise money for the environment. In Year 7 she put leaflets in the school tuckshop about the evils of junk food.

'Justine Fern did all that stuff, too,' Alyce said when I tried to talk to her about it last month. 'She's just as smart as me. Why don't kids pick on her?'

Justine knows what every other person in the world does. Open yourself up as much as Alyce has over the years and you're an easy target for people who are out to make themselves look better by making someone else look stupid. Alyce gave away the key to herself years ago. And she never changed the locks.

I couldn't tell her that, though. It would hurt too much. 'Justine Fern had the body of a twenty-one year old when she was five,' I said instead. And Alyce nodded sadly in agreement. It was mostly truth. With about three-quarters' worth of lies mixed in.

I can't tell you what happened between Alyce and Flemming in the library today because I wasn't there. What I can tell you is what happens after. Flemming turns up for practice half an hour late.

'You think you can waltz in here whenever you feel like it?' Coach yells. 'We've got our first big match at the end of this week. Give me five laps. Plus the five that everybody here on time has already done.'

Flemming smiles the whole ten laps.

'Doesn't prove a thing, Faltrain,' Martin says.

But it does.

I have this feeling tonight that things are on the up. Alyce has made a tiny step towards Flemming. Martin doesn't know it, but he's stepping towards his mum. And on Saturday, we're going to show everyone who thinks that the tryouts were rigged that they're wrong. Watch out, Firsts. Here comes Gracie Faltrain.

20

The only good Faltrain is a dead Faltrain.
Dan Woodbury

'Hey,' Woodbury says to me after his team wins the toss on Saturday. 'You may as well stay on that bench. You don't stand a chance.'

I can't believe this guy. Even I know the definition of denial. 'It's not like I haven't beaten you at least twice before, Woodbury.'

'And you're going to pay for it today.'

'What, angry that a girl's better than you?'

His face crumples like a used chip packet. His fists clench. 'I don't care that you're a girl. I care that you're a . . .'

'Hey.' Flemming walks over. 'Ref says we're about to start.'

The whistle goes and there's no more time for talk. The crowd roars. I tune everything out. My voice is the only one that matters, the only one I trust. I listen to that. And focus on the game.

I steal the ball from Woodbury and run towards goal. I sweep to the left and then to the right. I kick to Flemming who kicks to Corelli who passes to King. He shoots for goal.

Flemming's voice whoops through the crowd. Us one. Them none. 'Get used to it, Woodbury,' I say.

I love to win. I love the sound of cheers. I love the thumping in my chest. I love it all. We've got a perfect system. I'm too fast at the kick-off to be stopped. Flemming's too fast at the pass. Corelli's just too unpredictable. And we've all had six years at predicting him. We're strong. So strong there's only one way to stop us. Unfortunately, we don't see what that is until it's way too late.

They start their plan a minute before the second half begins. Martin is the first to go. It's brilliant; even I have to admit it. He's a sitting target in the goal. All they do is kick the ball hard at him before the whistle. The ball's not in play so Martin doesn't have to defend, but he acts on reflex. He's not expecting the kick and his timing is off. It hits him right between his fingers. From the middle of the field I hear the bone pop.

The whole team runs towards him. 'Probably just a dislocation,' the first-aid guy says to Coach. 'He's off, though.'

This is war, I think as Martin walks over to the bench. No one dislocates any part of Gracie Faltrain's boyfriend if they want to live.

'Shame about Knight,' Woodbury says while we're waiting for the second half to start. 'Accidents happen, though.'

'There are eleven accidents in this game. And not one of them is Martin.'

The whistle goes. Woodbury's on me like a coat in summer, heavy and thick and suffocating. He runs so close we're blurred. Flemming kicks the ball high in my direction. It curves across the sky. I shake off Woodbury and sprint towards it. But not for long.

I reach the ball just as he narrows the gap between us. His

fist thumps into my ribs and my scream cracks the day. I stumble forwards, spitting the ball loose like he's given me the Heimlich manoeuvre. My hands hit the ground, and then my head. My bones feel like glass under my skin.

I'm on the grass, desperately trying to catch my breath, when Woodbury kneels down beside me, his voice loud enough for the ref to hear. 'Are you okay, Faltrain?'

'That the only way you can win?' I manage to get out. 'Are you happy now?'

'Not really,' he whispers. 'I was aiming a little higher.'

There isn't time to answer him. His face tangles with the sky. And I don't remember anything else.

'We lost,' Flemming says, sitting next to my bed in the hospital while Mum and Dad talk to the doctors. 'By three goals.' I'm not sure what hurts him more, those words or the big black eye he's wearing.

'What I don't get,' I say, 'is how the referee didn't card Woodbury for knocking me out.'

'Gracie, Dan Woodbury and the referee were in parallel with each other. His vision was running along a 180-degree line, completely impaired,' Alyce says.

'Huh?' Flemming looks at her through his good eye.

'Woodbury put his back to the ref and blocked his view,' I translate Alyce-speak for everyone. 'So what happened to you?' I ask Flemming.

'Tom Dawson hit me about ten minutes after you passed out. He got sent off but they didn't care. With you and me and Martin off the field, they'd won the game and they knew it.'

'I can't even remember being carried away.'

Martin suddenly finds his strapped fingers very interesting. Alyce pulls out her book. Flemming checks his eye again in the mirror.

'Tell me she didn't. Tell me my mum didn't run onto the field and carry me off.'

'Sorry, Faltrain,' Martin says. 'It could have been worse, though.'

'How? How could it have been worse unless my dad came running on after her and told Dan Woodbury to stay away from his baby?'

There are a few seconds' silence out of respect for my dead reputation.

'At least I was unconscious.' I should look nice and relaxed in those pictures the reporters were taking.

'Cheer up,' Flemming says. 'Corelli's down the hall getting stitches in his leg and Francavilla is having two in his fist.'

'They hurt his fist?'

'He cut it on their defence's teeth after Corelli got kicked in the leg. He's out for the next game.'

'What about you, Martin?' I ask. 'Can you play next week?'

'Yep. I was lucky. They're only dislocated.'

'Sounds like I missed a good game of soccer.'

'They weren't playing soccer out there, Faltrain,' Martin says after Flemming and Alyce leave. 'They were playing us.'

'So next time we go in harder.' My bruised rib and wrist ripen like fruit as I speak.

'Harder than a dislocated finger, a sprained wrist, bruised rib, black eye, two sets of stitches . . .'

'Enough, Martin.'

'You were lucky Woodbury didn't break anything.'

'I get it, okay?' Every bone in my body gets it.

'My mum said something once that I've never forgotten. I was in Year 4 but they'd put me in the Year 5 team. A few of the kids had a bit of a go at me, for getting ahead of myself. "Marty," Mum said to me, "there'll always be people like that. People who want more than they've got so they take a little from everyone around." I remember thinking they'd only be able to take it from kids who let them, weak kids. "No, Marty, you're wrong," she said. "They try to take it from the strong ones. Because those people have the most of what they want." '

'So they want to take what we've got but we won't let them.'

'I wasn't talking about them taking from us,' Martin says. 'It was the other way round in the summer competition. We made them angry because that's how we played. And now we're paying for it.'

'We played to win, Martin.'

'And we loved every minute of it.'

'We didn't deserve what happened to us today. We did our best in the off-season games – there's nothing wrong with that. We followed the rules.'

'Well, it looks like the rules have changed, Faltrain.' And he waves goodbye with bandaged fingers. 'Now let's see how you like them.'

It's a sad team that gathers before Coach at practice on Monday. A black and blue and bruised team.

'We took a beating on Saturday, it's true. A hard, harsh, brutal beating.' Coach walks like he's the one who took the hits. 'But we can get up again.' He raises his hand in a fist and then opens it, like he's letting a bird free. Except he realises that there's nothing in it but air.

'We were up against guys playing dirty,' Flemming says. 'Next time it'll be a different team.'

'They'll play the same,' Corelli says. 'You heard them.'

'Heard what?' I ask. No one answers. 'Heard what?'

'After the match was over, Woodbury told Knight to get used to it. That every team hated us for how we played in the off-season games. That no one was going to be humiliated this season when the final is televised and scouts are on the lookout for state players,' Flemming finally tells me.

'They won't get away with playing like that every match,' I say.

'They got away with it last time,' Francavilla answers. 'I'm the one who's on the bench for a week.'

'The point is,' Martin says, 'even if they don't take us out, it's a harder match. Those guys are stronger than most of us and they're not scared to knock us down.'

The whole time our team is kicking back and forth the reasons why we're going to lose on Saturday, I'm getting angrier. 'We beat every one of those teams in the off-season games. We can do it again.'

'Maybe you don't remember all of the last match, Faltrain, on account of you being unconscious, but they had no trouble beating us,' Corelli says.

'This time it'll be different,' I answer.

'Oh yeah?' Francavilla asks. 'And how's that?'

'Because this time, we'll be ready for them; we'll train harder.' If there's one thing Gracie Faltrain doesn't do, it's back down. I won't be beaten by Dan Woodbury or anyone else. Some things a person can't walk away from. If we don't play in the Firsts competition this season then we'll never be able to look each other in the eye again. I'd rather stare at Flemming's black eye than at no eyes at all. I know how Corelli's feeling today because I feel it too. But giving up is the same as letting them beat you, and I'd rather go down on the field than on the sidelines. I'd rather go out fighting.

'Training harder won't make a difference,' Flemming says.

'What's our other option – quit after one game?' I ask.

Flemming punches his hand quietly against his leg. 'I didn't say I wanted to quit.'

'Then let's stop talking and start working,' Martin says.

We push ourselves tonight, even though we're hurting. I kick the ball hard at Martin. He slams it back, favouring his good hand.

'We're not going to win on Saturday,' Flemming says to me after practice while we wait for Martin to finish packing his stuff. 'Not unless we change the way we play.' He picks at the dirt stuck to his shoes.

'What do you mean?' I ask.

He flicks his eyes behind me.

'What's up?' Martin asks, slinging his bag over his shoulder.

'Nothing,' I say, and grab his hand.

Flemming leaves us at the end of his street. But his words stay with me long after he disappears.

I flick through the weekend paper tonight before I go to sleep. My ad for Mrs Knight is in the classifieds section. Please let her find it, I think. Martin needs some luck. He needs to win. I cut out the tiny box and keep it. Martin might want to remember, one day, where the best part of his life started.

21

Boy meets girl. Girl meets ground.
Local News Weekly

'That's kind of funny,' Corelli says, looking at the headline from one of the local papers on Tuesday before practice.

'Yeah, it's hilarious. Have you read the article?' I grab the paper off him. 'Declan Corelli cried like a baby after he was kicked in the leg . . .'

'It doesn't say that.'

'No. But a picture is worth a thousand words.' I turn the page to the shot of Corelli being carried off the field. 'Not so funny now, is it?'

'It's humiliating for all of us,' Flemming snarls, and snatches the paper. 'But it won't happen again. We have to win on Saturday.'

'We will,' I say, 'no problem.'

A page of the paper blows from his hand before he can catch it. He throws the rest on the ground.

'They took us by surprise last week,' I tell him. 'This Saturday, we'll be ready.'

22

Gracie, that colour really suits you.
You look so good wearing the ground
on your face.
Annabelle Orion

'That guy wasn't in the off-season games,' I say, looking at number nine from the opposition this Saturday. 'I would have remembered him.'

'He can't be in Year 12,' Corelli answers.

'Rumour has it he was kept down,' Francavilla says, making himself comfortable on the bench. 'For ten years. They call him Truck.'

'Good name.' I can't stop staring at him, mainly because he can't stop staring at me.

'Is it just my imagination, or does he seem kind of fixated on Faltrain?' Flemming asks.

Truck points in my direction and draws a hand across his throat. 'I don't think it's just you,' I say as I watch him do it.

'You should sit this one out, Faltrain, at least for the first half till we know what we're up against,' Martin says.

'No way. With Francavilla out, you need me.'

'Stick close to Flemming then. I've got a bad feeling about this.'

The sun disappears behind the clouds as the whistle goes. I take off after the ball and concentrate on playing. The other team concentrates on me. Truck speeds up behind me, gaining as I run towards goal. 'Get out of the way, girlie,' he yells as he overtakes.

'*Girlie*?' I'll show you who's a girlie. Guys like Truck pick on kids they think are weak. I heard him taunting Corelli earlier about his crap kicks. He has a point there, but being a girl doesn't make you weak. Being a girl doesn't leave you vulnerable on the field.

'Faltrain!' Flemming calls as Truck does a three-point turn and slams into me. 'Watch out!'

I'd like to think that Truck wasn't aiming for my boob. I'd really like to believe, like the ref obviously does, that he knocked me in the heat of the moment. But I know my boobs. They're not all that big. You really have to look for them.

'Time,' Coach shouts, and runs towards me. The team crowds around.

'That had to hurt,' Corelli says.

'You'd know,' Singh answers for me. I'm in too much pain to say anything.

'You need to swap with me,' Martin says. 'It's too rough out there.'

'Go goalie? No way.'

'Faltrain, I've never said it before, but I like everything, um, exactly where it is on you.'

'Believe me, Martin. So do I,' I answer, wishing I'd let Mum talk me into that padded bra last year. I drag myself to a standing position. 'Now, let's play.'

I'm only standing for about five minutes. I turn to see Truck racing towards me, elbows up. My normal instinct would be to run, to dodge him and keep moving towards the goal. But not today. I stand still, like a rabbit on the road. A rabbit with both paws covering her boobs for protection. Truck roars past me, just close enough to clip my chest. His momentum knocks me sideways, sending me flying, body bouncing on the ground like I'm landing on a trampoline.

'She's dead, Bill,' I hear Mum yelling at Dad, her face fuzzy in the background.

'She's not dead, Helen, she's still breathing.'

'Do rabbits even have boobs?' I hear myself say. My ears are ringing. Everything is as foggy as winter.

'She's got brain damage, Bill.'

The fog clears an inch, just enough to make things visible. I have boob damage, not brain damage. 'I think we should all stop talking now. And get me to a hospital.'

'He didn't even get carded, Martin?' I ask when I've regained the power of speech.

'The ref gave us an indirect free. But even to me it didn't look like he hit you on purpose, Faltrain.'

'It was sort of like you were a bug that got caught on his windshield by accident,' Flemming says.

'Great. I feel a whole lot better now. What did the other team say about me, after the match?'

'Nothing, Faltrain. Don't worry about it,' Martin says.

'Who cares what a pack of losers say, anyway?' Flemming pats my shoulder lightly, like I'm a dog that might bite him.

'Martin, either you tell me now, or when I'm better I'll aim for that ball I missed when you lied the last time.'

'They said, how could they have been deliberately aiming for your chest . . .' Martin's voice crumbles like a biscuit.

'What?'

'They said,' he takes a big breath and the words sprint out of his mouth, 'how could they aim for your chest when there's nothing there, anyway.'

'Just for the record, Faltrain,' Flemming says, 'we all think you've got quite a nice set of . . .'

'Get out,' I cut him off. 'Or you two won't have a nice set of anything.'

Just then Alyce walks through the door with a box of chocolates. On a scale of one to ten of how happy I am to see her, I'd score me at about eleven. 'Thanks for coming, Alyce.'

'Yes, thanks for coming,' Flemming says, taking the chocolates out of her hands and ripping open the packet.

'I told you both to get out.'

Alyce sits on the end of my bed after they've gone and squeezes my hand.

'Everyone's talking about the size of my chest.'

'I know.'

'It's humiliating.'

'Gracie, they're not picking on you because you're a girl.'

'Tell that to my boobs, Alyce.'

'They're picking on the thing that's different about you. Corelli got harassed just as much for not being the greatest kicker. Andrew was picked on till he hit back. They're attacking because they're scared, Gracie. They don't want to lose again.'

Alyce has good advice, and I feel better that she's here. But I'd give anything for Jane to call or email. I'd give anything to know what she'd say to me. Maybe it's the concussion, but her voice isn't even an echo today. I want to tell Alyce how much I miss Jane, but somehow I feel like it would hurt her.

'Look on the bright side,' Alyce says. 'They still didn't manage to break anything. It's only a mild concussion. The doctor told your parents you only need to miss one game.'

And on what planet is that a bright side, Alyce?

23

C squared equals A squared
plus B squared.
Alyce Fuller

A has been square long enough.
It's time to break some rules.
Gracie Faltrain

I guess Alyce has had a lot of practice looking for the bright side in pitch darkness. I mean, ever since I can remember no one has really liked her. She's fruit. It's sweet if you try it, but who picks an apple when there are a hundred different chocolate bars to choose from?

I walk in on her and Flemming in the classroom on Tuesday morning. It's two minutes before the bell goes. Flemming is never early for class. 'Timing's everything, Faltrain,' he always says at soccer practice. 'Don't shoot too early. Don't shoot too late.'

Alyce is smiling like she's found a book she really wants to read. Flemming is laughing like he does when he kicks a goal. The two of them jump as I thump my books on the table. 'Didn't mean to interrupt.'

'I was just helping Andrew with the body of his essay,' Alyce says. 'It's very good.' I'm sure you think so, Alyce. I don't say that, though. She looks embarrassed enough.

'Thanks,' Flemming mumbles, and moves his stuff to the back of the room where he always sits.

This is the big problem with Flemming and Alyce getting it together. There are patterns at school that are hard to break. Kids like Flemming sit up the back and swing on their chairs. They play footy or soccer or cricket at lunchtime. They need a map to get to the library. And one thing I can guarantee – girls like Alyce? They're not on the map.

The bell goes and the rest of the kids drift in. Annabelle and Susan sit next to Flemming. They make jokes and he laughs, leans back on his chair and becomes the guy I know on the soccer field. Alyce hunches over and becomes invisible again. He starts to stuff around and she takes out her book and neatly rules her page. I look across at it: lines and lines of sums, all with tiny ticks next to them.

'The class hasn't even started yet, nerd,' Annabelle says, throwing a ball of paper at the back of Alyce's head.

'Get lost,' I yell back at her.

Flemming says nothing. And it's louder than all the shouts in the room.

'All right, everyone.' Mrs Hinter comes in. 'Let's pick up where we left off yesterday, exercise 3c, left-hand side this time.'

'Alyce, what's the formula for finding the hypotenuse, again?' I ask.

'C squared equals A squared plus B squared.'

'How come you're so good at maths?'

'It's easy, Gracie. Just follow the formula, follow the pattern and you get the right answer.' She leans over my page. 'There,' she points. 'You've put this in the wrong order.'

'Why does C squared have to equal A squared plus B squared, anyway?' I kick at the chair in front of me.

'It just does, Gracie. That's the way things are.'

'Maybe I'm not going to follow that rule.'

'Then your answer will be wrong.' Mrs Hinter comes up behind me. 'And you will fail the test.'

I look over at Flemming laughing with Annabelle. He doesn't seem half as happy as he did when he was alone with Alyce. Some rules are meant to be broken. Because if you don't, then nothing ever changes.

'So why aren't you sitting with your girlfriend?' Annabelle asks Flemming while Alyce is up the front getting help. The thing about people like Annabelle is that not only do they have access to information, but they know how to use it.

'Fuller's not my girlfriend. She's helping me study, that's all.'

'So you're not asking her to the dance?'

'Yeah, right,' he says.

At least Alyce isn't around to hear. Flemming should stand up for her, but the way things are, he'd be reversing the laws of the universe. The world would spin backwards. Alyce is worth a hundred Annabelles. But even I have to admit, if the world ever spun backwards, everyone on it would be sick.

I have to get Alyce to do something to change where she fits in. Then there won't be a problem with her and Flemming. She has to show off her talents to everyone in the school. Her talent is being smart. All she needs is more exposure, like those mice, and she'll be sunning it up with the likes of Annabelle.

'Why don't you join in the comedy debate this year?' I ask her after class. 'Everyone in the school will be watching.'

'You've just answered your own question.'

'Alyce you're funny and you're smart. You'd be great.'

'No.'

'Annabelle goes in it every year. It'd be the perfect chance to get her back.'

'Gracie, I'm not interested in getting Annabelle back.'

'Fine. Be a mouse all your life. That's why Flemming doesn't talk to you when the other kids are around. He never will unless you show him what you're really made of.'

It's harsh, I know, but sometimes you have to be cruel to be kind. Alyce looks like I've punched her in the stomach and knocked the air right out of her. She looks like how I felt on Saturday. But I'm going back in there as soon as I can and she has to as well.

'Andrew doesn't talk to me when people are around because he sees exactly what I'm made of,' she says. 'And he's embarrassed.'

Then prove him wrong, I think after she walks away. I write her name on the list for comedy debaters. Better yet, let me prove it for you.

24

'Nice pictures, Faltrain,' Flemming says.
'That's funny,' I tell him. 'Come here
and let me kick you in the balls.
Then we'll swap some jokes.'
Gracie Faltrain

Proving yourself is part of the game. If you stop trying to do that, then it's over. I guess by that definition, Alyce's game never really started. For as long as I've known her, she has never tried to show people like Annabelle that she's worth something. And take it from me, that's a green light for Annabelle to run right over the top of Alyce.

'Why go to practice, Gracie?' Annabelle asks me before training on Wednesday. 'You're already so good at getting your brains knocked out.'

'You might keep your brains here,' I point to my chest. 'Me? I like to keep them in my head, Annabelle.'

'I thought you might want a copy of this,' she calls before I walk off. She's waving another edition of the local paper at me. 'For your photo album.'

I take it from her carefully, like a bomb that might go off in my face. My heart slides a bit further down my chest with every page I turn. By the time I get to the report on the Firsts game, it's lying on the ground next to my shoes.

'Nice picture,' Annabelle says, grinding it under her foot.

Whoever took the photos has a knack for action. In the first one I'm standing with two hands clamped over my chest. In the second Truck is collecting me on his windshield. In the third I'm flying through the air and by the fourth I'm flat on my back. If you cut them out and flicked the pages really quickly, you'd have one of those comics where you can make the person move. A mini action replay. I close my eyes at the thought of all the Firsts teams flicking me backwards and forwards. Hands over my boobs. Hands off. Annabelle's laugh is the pitch of nails scraped down a blackboard.

The team's sitting on the ground, staring at their hands or their feet, when I come around the corner. Each one of us has at least two major bruises clearly visible. And if they're like me? They've got at least three in places that the rest of us will never see.

'Right!' Coach yells, and swishes his feet across the grass. 'Right.' For the first time since I've known him, Coach has absolutely no idea what to say. I mean, what are his choices? You're a pack of losers and there's nothing but humiliation ahead for the rest of the season? He does the same as every other teacher when they're stuck for words. He makes us answer the question.

'Flemming, what happened out there on Saturday?'

'We got beaten. Again.'

Understatement of the year.

'We'd need to be on steroids to beat those teams,' Corelli says.

'You'd be a danger to yourself on drugs,' Flemming shoots back.

'Shut up. You weren't so smart on Saturday with your face pressed into the dirt.'

'What?' Flemming stands up and walks over to him. 'You want to be on steroids? Fine, go ask your mother where she gets hers from.'

They're not the only two who are angry. Any second now the whole team could erupt. It's easier to be mad with the person next to you than with yourself. We're all searching for a way to feel better about what happened on Saturday. We're all after someone to blame.

'Sit down, you two,' Martin says, still on the ground. He raises his eyes to them, but not his voice. There's a staring match for maybe five full seconds and then they crouch back down on the grass. Martin hardly ever tells people what to do. But when he does, you listen.

'We lost on Saturday because they needed us to. We humiliated everyone in the off-season games and they wanted us to feel it. They're playing rough.'

'They're playing unfair.' Singh punches at the air.

'Yeah, they are. But we're still the best team in the league. So we practise harder and we get so good they can't beat us.'

'You really think that's going to work?' Flemming rips grass from the ground.

I can't believe in two games we've gone from being the best to being scared enough to walk away because of players like Dan Woodbury. He's nowhere near as good as me, or Martin or Flemming. He's just rougher.

'They've got us running scared because none of them are afraid to break the rules,' I say.

'They've got us running scared because none of them are afraid to break noses,' Francavilla says.

Coach is quiet while we talk. He knows he can't send us back into battle. It has to be our decision. 'You all look too tired for training tonight, anyway. Think about whether you want to stay in the competition. We'll vote on it tomorrow. There's no shame in pulling out,' he says, and then shuffles slowly back to his office.

'I'm not pulling out.' Flemming is the first to speak. 'There's no way I'm letting those guys take away my chance at playing for the state.'

I know why he's so angry. He's like me. Soccer is the only thing that makes him feel good when he gets an F on his work. It's the only reason he drags himself out of bed in the morning and through the day at school. What happens to him if he loses that?

'I'm not pulling out, either. And I've got more reason than the rest of you guys to walk away. They target me because I'm a girl.'

'If we keep going, it could be more humiliating than pulling out,' Corelli says. Francavilla and Singh nod.

'It doesn't have to be,' Flemming answers, his eyes focused on the dirty ground.

Everyone waits for him to speak again. We all know what he means, but no one wants to be the first to suggest it.

'All I'm saying is a person should be able to defend themself. It's our right. If we play again and don't do that, one of us is going to get hurt. Really hurt. Is that what you all want?'

When Flemming puts it like that, it's hard to say yes. I've played with these guys since Year 7. I won't stand by and watch them hospitalised.

'We haven't done anything to deserve what they're doing to us.' Flemming's voice gets louder. 'So it's agreed, then. On Saturday we defend ourselves.' Everyone nods except Martin. He's walking away.

'Martin,' I call. 'Wait up.'

He slows down. 'Tell me you didn't agree with Flemming.'

'You don't think we've got the right to defend ourselves?' I can tell he wants to say something, but he's holding it back. 'What, Martin?'

'I was just thinking about Woodbury and his team. They've never played like this before.'

'So? They're playing like it now,' I answer.

'Yeah. And I was just wondering what Woodbury said to his team to convince them it was okay to fight dirty. Did he tell them it was self-defence after the way we treated them in the off-season games?'

'We didn't try to hurt them. We didn't break any rules.'

'No. Because that would have been wrong, wouldn't it, Faltrain?' He shakes his head and walks off.

It's not that clear-cut when you're on the field, though. It's easy for Martin to say stuff like that. He's safer in goal; there's less chance of him being knocked to the ground in there. Martin didn't finish the last game with the taste of dirt in his mouth. That taste changes things. Believe me.

25

Fair enough, fighting's wrong.
But fighting back? That's a
whole different ball game.
Gracie Faltrain

Alyce gives me that half smile of hers when I sit next to her in science on Thursday.

'I'm not putting my name down for the debate, Gracie,' she says.

'Fair enough.' No need to put it down twice.

'Right, class.' Mrs Turner's voice stops us talking. 'We're moving on to a new topic today: The Beginnings of the Universe.' She starts passing out a worksheet and everyone starts talking.

'Did Flemming tell you about the plan?' I ask.

'He said you are going to play to protect yourselves.' Alyce straightens her glasses and neatens her skirt.

'And you don't agree?'

'I didn't say that.'

'No, but you think it, I can tell. You saw the paper, Alyce. I was humiliated in that last match.'

'And you've complained about how unfair it was ever since.'

'So?'

'So what makes it right now that you're doing it?'

'It's us.'

'Alyce and Gracie,' Mrs Turner says, 'stop talking and start on the questions.'

Alyce looks at her sheet. 'Read the article and explain, in your own words or through pictures, how man developed from the beginning of time.'

'They don't want much,' I say. 'Explain in twenty-five words or less how the world has changed in a billion years.'

'It's not hard, Gracie,' Alyce says, drawing a star, an amoeba and an ape. 'We haven't really changed that much at all.'

26

There are only two types of players on
that field. Us and them.
Andrew Flemming

'I did a bit of research,' Francavilla says on Saturday morning. 'Their best player is a guy called David Trentham. Ham for short. A mate of mine from their school says he was bragging about taking Faltrain out in the first minute.'

'Yeah, well, he's lucky I'm not playing today.'

'He'll go for the rest of us when he sees she's injured,' Flemming says. 'So we do like we said, and eliminate the threat. Agreed?' Everyone nods, except Martin.

The plan is to take out Ham, the strongest member of the opposition, in the first five minutes of the game. 'After that,' Flemming says before Coach arrives, 'we won't have to do anything else. They'll know we mean business.'

'And if things don't go like you've planned?' Martin asks.

'They will,' Flemming answers.

'What makes you think they won't?' I ask Martin before the match starts.

'Unless they're dead, Faltrain, most people try to get up again.'

The whistle goes and I take my seat on the bench. Corelli's next to Ham. Francavilla is on the left of the field. Singh is standing on the right. King and Wrecker are near the ref, ready to create a diversion if we need it.

Once the ball is in play, Flemming sets up the hit. He kicks to Corelli, Corelli misses, nothing suspicious there, and as soon as Ham has possession Francavilla and Singh run in from opposite sides of the field and body slam him. He hits the ground quick and hard.

'Well, will you look over there,' I say as the ref gives them a free kick. 'It's a Ham sandwich.'

'A walking sandwich,' the guy behind me says.

Like the lead in a horror movie Ham clicks his neck back into place and goes straight up to Francavilla. He doesn't even bother to lower his voice. 'You're dead,' he says.

Don't look now, everyone, but things aren't going exactly as we planned. Martin's thinking the same thing. Worry is splashed across his face like paint. I have a feeling things are about to get messy out there.

Play starts again and the opposition runs close to us, testing us. It's like they're at a market, shopping for fruit. Everyone's looking for the softest, sweetest piece to pick. Ten minutes before half time, Ham finds his.

Corelli takes possession to the left of our goal. In a second he's surrounded by a scrabbling pack of players, seagulls screaming for the ball like it's a chip on the beach. Francavilla runs towards the crowd and dives in. He swims around for a bit, elbowing his way to Corelli. Someone kicks the ball out and the whole pack scatters. Except for Declan. And I use his first name out of respect for the almost dead. He sinks like a lilo after the holidays.

Something changes after he's carried off. I can feel it. There's a smell of metal in the air, a smell of blood. And everyone on our team starts circling, trying to find it. They're hungry. And they're sick of being fed on.

Flemming slides across to the ball and shoulders one of their strikers to the ground. The ref's not looking so he claims it as his own and starts running. Francavilla coasts along beside him, his arms half out, clearing the way.

'What the hell are they doing out there, Faltrain?' Coach asks, shaking his head as Singh sinks his foot into some guy's knee.

'Just a rough game, I guess.' Singh doesn't care who he hurts, I think, and excitement grabs at my throat.

'Looks like we might win,' I say.

Coach grunts. 'Depends on how you define the word.'

There's twenty times the fun out there, today. There's twenty times the blood. We thrash them. Five goals to one. That's what I call winning. And I've never wanted to be out there more.

Coach is quiet after the game. 'I'll talk to you all in two weeks, after the term holidays,' he tells us. And then he packs up his things and leaves.

'A few more games like that and we'll be on our way to the finals,' Flemming says after he's gone.

'You're not talking about self defence now, though, are you?' Martin asks. He's staring everyone in the eyes, willing us to look back. Even I can't do that. The only way I can survive on that field is if the team plays like they did today.

'We were still defending ourselves. We were just getting in there first,' Flemming says, the only one of us looking straight back at him.

'You cheated. Is that how you want to play?' The two of them remind me of dogs, baring their teeth for a fight.

'I want to win,' Flemming says. 'Don't you?'

'Not like that.'

'You're not out there, though, are you? You're in goal.'

'Shut up, Flemming, Martin's as much in the team as the rest of us,' I say, and Maiden nods from the side.

'Fine. I reckon we should vote, then.'

'Okay,' Martin says. 'Who thinks we should sink to the other teams' level?' Slowly, everyone raises their hand except for him. I raise mine too.

'Right then,' he says, looking at me. 'At least I understand how the game works now. I reckon it's time for a new captain. I don't want to be in charge of a team like this.'

Flemming nods. 'Are you still playing?'

No one talks. No one moves.

'I won't play dirty, but I'm still in.'

'You can't sit back and let us do all the work . . .' Flemming starts, but Martin turns on him. His face bunches into a snarl.

'Don't tell me how to play,' he says, walking off.

'No one says a word to Coach,' Flemming says, taking the lead now. 'What he doesn't know can't hurt him.'

I watch them all walk back to the change rooms under a dirty sky. It's raining as I leave. The only sound is my feet on the grass, muddy and wet by the time I arrive at the edge of the field.

Part of the reason I love Martin is that he wouldn't play like Woodbury, no matter how hard the game. But if we don't, then the bad guys win. They punch your boobs and knock you out because you're not brave enough to stop them.

I know I won't sleep tonight unless I talk to Martin first. I need to explain to him why I voted the way I did. That if we don't fight to win, if we accept things the way they are, then it's like we're saying that losing is good enough.

Mr Knight isn't on the porch. The curtains are edged with light, so I know they're home. I knock and wait for Martin to open the door.

'Can I come in?'

He looks over his shoulder. 'It's not a great time. Wait here for a second while I get my coat. I'll walk you home.'

I can hear the clatter of plates from the kitchen. I edge my way down the hall. Mr Knight's clearing the table. He's wearing a suit and tie instead of a tracksuit. He looks at me with red and tired eyes. 'Hello, Gracie. Stay for dessert?'

I'm nodding as Martin walks back in, zipping up his coat.

'Where's Karen?' I ask as we eat.

'She's at a friend's house tonight,' Mr Knight answers. There's quiet for a bit after this, just the clicking of spoons against bowls.

'I look pretty snazzy today, don't you think, Gracie?' Mr Knight's smile is like Martin's. His eyes are deeper, though, sad and sinking like a tired swimmer. This year Martin's eyes have started tipping in like that.

'You do look pretty snazzy. What's the occasion?'

'I went for a job interview.'

'Did you get it?'

'I think maybe I did.'

'What's the job?'

'It's at the local shopping centre. I'll be the new cleaner.'

Martin looks at me, fierce, guarding something he thinks I'll steal. 'That's great, Mr Knight,' I say. 'So I guess this is a celebration.'

***

'Why did you look at me like that?' I ask on the way home.

'Like what?'

'You know. When your dad told me about his job, you thought I'd say something to make him feel bad.'

'It passed through your eyes, Faltrain. You felt sorry for him. You feel sorry for my whole family.'

'I don't.' But I'm lying. My body feels heavier when I walk into that house.

'He's happier than I've ever seen him – or at least he's pretending to be; that's what matters.'

'And what about you? How long can you keep pretending for?'

Martin's a shadow in the dark street. I can barely see where his voice is coming from. 'I asked him last year to take some notice of me, and he is.'

'Is that enough?' I ask.

'Most of the time.' Martin struggles to get the words out, like they're all crowded in his throat, pushing against each other. 'I think there are some parts of me that'll never be happy, because of stuff that happened with Mum, but I can't change that, so it's better for all of us to not think about it.'

'You mean it's better for your dad?'

'I mean it's better for all of us. What did you come over for, anyway?' he asks as we reach my door.

'I wanted to explain why I voted against you.'

'Faltrain, I wish you hadn't, but I'd have bet a million dollars today that you'd vote the way you did.'

'And you don't care?'

He shrugs. 'You play how you live. I can't change that.'

'We'll lose if we don't do what Flemming says.'

'My mum always said, "There are a million ways to lose, Marty. And half of them make you feel like you're winning."'

I can't wait till I find Mrs Knight. Then I can ask her what the hell that means.

27

Stop panting, Corelli. They're not real.
Gracie Faltrain

When we get back from holidays, we have two practices every night: one with Coach and one in the park around the corner from school.

'Okay, so everyone's clear on how we're playing tomorrow,' Flemming says on Friday afternoon before our next match. 'We can't afford to lose players, so if you hit them, do it when no one's looking. Elbows out and when you run, run hard. Remember, protect Faltrain. Keep her clear to kick goals.'

'Don't worry about me.'

'Faltrain, you're half their size,' Flemming says.

'Perfect. I'm exactly at ball height.'

The whole team crosses their legs. Corelli moves his hands over his front. I'm making everyone pay tomorrow. Watch out. Here comes goal-kicking, head-kicking, ball-kicking Gracie Faltrain.

'I have two words for you,' Mum says when I get home from practice.

'You can tell me to pull out as much as you like; I'm playing tomorrow.'

'"Pull out" aren't my two words. Mine are: "boob protectors".'

'What?'

'Well, that's not their official name,' she says, and holds up the mother of all padded bras.

'I can't wear that, Mum. I can't walk onto the ground looking like Pamela Anderson.'

'I don't care how you walk on, but I want you walking off like Pamela, not Patrick Anderson.'

'Who's he?'

'Whoever he is, Gracie, he is flat-chested.'

'Hand that thing over.'

It takes a while for Mum to strap me in. I check myself out in the mirror. 'I don't look half bad.'

'I have more protection.' She pulls out guards I never knew existed.

'Ear guards?'

'I've heard of players having their ears ripped off.'

'Mum, I'll be fine.'

'You're all I've got, Gracie Faltrain.' She tries to pull me close but the protectors stop her halfway. 'So be careful out there.'

'Don't worry about me. Worry about the others. By the way, did Jane call?'

'No. Why don't you ring her? The longer you put off calling after a fight, the harder it is.'

'I know. I'll ring her after the match tomorrow.'

Part of me is putting it off because I'm hoping that she'll call me. I want things to be the way they were. It feels like this is the final test for us. I don't tell Mum, but I tested Jane after her cousin, Josie, left, too. I was just a little bit quieter than usual at school.

'Faltrain, you're not still angry about Josie? You're my best friend, you idiot.' It felt so good to hear her say it. Like drinking warm soup when you've got a cold.

If Jane doesn't ring to wish me luck, then I guess I'll have proof. She really is forgetting me.

I look up into the stands just before the whistle goes and see Mum and Dad and Alyce waving.

'You don't have to go out there again, baby,' Dad said on the way. 'You've got nothing to prove.'

'I'm playing.'

'Then wear the protection I bought for you,' Mum said. 'And never be ashamed to run.'

I've left most of the guards on the side of the field. If I wore them all I'd look like the Michelin Man. I have got the boob protectors on, though. I'm feeling kind of womanly out here today.

Alyce gives me the thumbs-up. It's good to have her here, even though I know she doesn't agree with me. I block out the thought that Jane hasn't even sent me a text. There's no time to get soppy. It's kill or be killed. And I am too young to die.

'Make me proud,' Coach says before we run on. 'Play hard. Play fair.' What's fair, though? Is it fair to kick the guy who kicked you a second before? Coach isn't on the field. He's not the one walking into a war. The opposition is looking at us like we're Christmas presents. Unless we fight they'll rip us open.

'Stay moving, stay conscious,' Flemming said to me at practice. The plan is for me to work with Maiden. He clears anything that gets in my way. I kick the ball clear into goal.

The two of us power down the field after kick-off. Maiden sees the ball and slams the guy who's kicking it. He sends it my way and I run, as fast as I can. I dodge around players and feast on their looks of surprise. I make it to the goal with only one player at my back. I hear the sound of Corelli tripping over him. He's the perfect accident. I have all the space I need to kick and score.

Soccer's so much easier when you don't have to rely on skill. Maiden, Francavilla, Singh and Flemming are my personal bulldozers, clearing the field of bodies so nothing stands in my way. The only problem is, I guess, bulldozers break down. They run out of petrol. They get held up in traffic. They crash. And then you're left trying to make your own way. On foot.

Things are fine until the last ten minutes of the second half. The score is three all. The next goal is the decider. Everyone's focused on Singh, who's about to throw the ball into play. It's only luck that makes me look across at Flemming. The striker standing next to him flips his arm up and smacks him right in the face.

I can't believe it. 'Did you see that?' I'm yelling as I run over. Flemming's holding his eye. The ref raises his hands as if to say, I didn't see anything. A slow grin spreads across the striker's face as Flemming sits on the bench. Don't smile too soon. You won't win if I have anything to do with it. You won't even tie.

Singh throws the ball. I take it. I look around for Maiden but he's surrounded by three of their players. Francavilla is shadowed by another. I'm on my own. There's a galloping storm of feet behind me as I run, thundering, desperate to catch up. There's a voice in the back of my head, and it's saying something like, 'If they catch you, you're dead.' It's not a very helpful voice. Gracie Faltrain, go, go, go. I'm going so fast all the breath in me is spent before I'm near the goal. I've got nothing left to pay for the shot.

The opposition crowds me. We're all tangled together, everyone knotted around the ball. I can't kick. There's not enough room. Any minute the whistle will sound. I'm so close, all I need is a tiny gap and we can win.

I flick my leg back as hard as I can and slam the player behind me right between the legs. He topples and pulls three of his mates with him. That's all the space I need. I smack the ball and watch it bounce at the back of the net. Oh yeah. Hear me roar.

They're all shouting at the ref, but he holds his hands up again. 'I couldn't see a thing,' he says. I get the feeling he's seen too much, today, and it's easier to block it out. But that's working in my favour this time, so who cares?

Our whole team is exploding with excitement. Except for Martin. 'Congratulations,' he says to me. 'Great goal.'

I don't have time to talk about it with him. 'Get your things and get in the car, Gracie Faltrain,' Mum says. 'You've got some explaining to do.'

'I have never been so ashamed in my life,' she shouts on the way home. Dad doesn't say much, but he nods along every now and then.

'I kicked the winning goal.'

'You kicked that boy in the balls, Gracie Faltrain. I saw it. Everyone did.'

'The ref didn't.'

'You think that's what matters?' She pulls the car into the driveway. 'Go to your room and stay there.' She sits staring straight ahead, waiting for me to move.

'We did what it took to win, Mum. Would you be happier if you were sitting in the hospital with me like before?'

'Get inside,' she says through gritted teeth. 'Before *I* put you in hospital.'

I don't care. I'd rather feel a little bit bad about myself and a lot good about winning than the other way around. They started it. They can't complain if we finish it off.

Mum barely talks to me all weekend. I'm grounded. No calls. No visitors. No nothing.

'Here,' she says, and throws the sports section of the local paper at me on Sunday. 'This is for you.' She walks into the garden and slams the back door.

'Girl Drives Ball Home', the headline reads.

That's kind of funny. And not a bad picture, if I do say so myself.

28

I've known Faltrain for eleven years. Once she gets up a bit of speed, she can talk about herself all year. Don't even bother butting in with your own problems. She'll run right over the top of you. And wonder what the bump was.
Jane Iranian

Jane finally calls on Sunday night. 'Hi, Faltrain.'

'Jane, hi.' If Mum catches me I'll get into trouble, but I have to share the game with someone. 'Wait'll you hear what happened in soccer.'

'Faltrain, I really need to talk to you about something.'

'This won't take long. And I could get thrown off the phone any second, so me first.' When Jane hears this she'll want to be friends with me again.

'I kicked the most amazing goal yesterday. I was surrounded by the opposition. Everyone thought there was no way I could make it. And then at the last minute I flipped my leg back and kicked this guy right where he lives. The whole pack of them toppled over.'

'You sound like you enjoyed it.'

'He deserved everything he got.'

'Why?'

'Because he was trying to stop me scoring the goal.'

'Isn't that the point, Faltrain?'

'They started it, Jane. You weren't there. You don't know what it was like.'

'You're right, Faltrain,' she says. 'I wasn't there.' Her voice dips in the middle like a lumpy couch.

'Are you mad at me?' I ask.

'No, I'm not mad. It just feels like we've changed, that's all.'

Here it comes. The kiss-off. The final nail in the coffin. The spin cycle of the washing machine. The last bite of the cake. Jane's about to tell me it's too hard being friends across all that ocean.

'Gracie Faltrain, get yourself back in your room. I told you before. You're grounded this weekend. That means no phone calls. No Martin. No nothing.'

Maybe you need to make that a little clearer, Mum. At least she's saved me from hearing Jane say the actual words. She doesn't need me anymore. It's over.

'Guess you have to go, then, Faltrain.'

'I guess I do.' Bye Jane. It was great while it lasted.

29

Me date Fuller?
Right, like I'd go out with a girl wearing
Orion's boot mark on her arse.
Andrew Flemming

It's time to face up to life the way things really are, Gracie Faltrain. Good things end. Someone always eats the last chocolate biscuit. Summer clouds over. Best friends leave. At least you still have Alyce.

'So, did you study with Flemming after the game on the weekend?' I ask on Monday morning.

'He didn't feel like it.'

'Oh.'

'We went out for dinner instead.' Her voice rises like keys on a piano. Annabelle can't help hearing.

'Really? Did you do anything afterwards?'

'We watched a DVD at my place,' Alyce answers, already edging away. I grab her arm. Not so fast, best buddy. You'll miss the show.

'What's going on?' Susan asks.

I'll handle this, I think. It's going to take a little delicacy.

'Alyce went out to dinner with Flemming on the weekend.' I say it loud so everyone hears. Flemming and Susan have one of those on again, off again things. At the moment they're off. And that's how I'm planning on keeping it.

I make my next move as casual as I can. 'So, Annabelle, I guess you're taking Dan to the dance. Susan, who are you going with?' Her mouth flat-lines as Mrs Tunnisi picks captains.

'Andrew and Susan, choose your teams.'

Flemming takes me and Singh and Corelli. He takes everyone he can except Alyce; her smile reminds me of a kite Dad bought me once that couldn't quite get off the ground. She's picked last, like always, and by Susan. Even then it's pretty clear she isn't on anybody's team. I give her shoulder a pat but she pulls away.

'Alyce?'

'We're starting, Gracie,' she says, and walks over to her position on the court. She looks beaten already.

I can't take my revenge on Annabelle, though. She tells Mrs Tunnisi she wants to start the game on the bench. 'What, scared of me beating you again?' I ask.

'You're on my team, loser.'

I'll never be on your team, Annabelle. You can bet on that.

I'm at the other end of the court when it happens. 'Alyce,' Susan calls, and signals for her to catch. The throw is the smallest bit too wide. The tiniest bit too far. Alyce has to chase it. Belinda Daly could easily reach the ball. But she doesn't. And that's how I know. It's a set-up.

'Alyce,' I yell, but she can't hear me. All her attention is focused on running. I've never seen her more determined to make it. I guess she figures with Flemming watching, she has something to prove.

I start to move but I'm too far away. Annabelle leans back on the bench and stretches her legs out lazily, like she's a million miles away. She knows exactly where she is. She's five steps from Alyce, who's approaching fast.

I watch one of the best friends I've got fly over Annabelle's legs and hit the concrete on all fours, like a dog begging. She's trying to get up when Annabelle lands her foot on her arse and pushes her over again. It wasn't exactly what I had in mind when I said Alyce's destiny needed a bit of a kick.

Every kid in the class claps and shouts except for me. Flemming laughs like it's stuck in his throat. He laughs like his eyes don't know what his mouth's doing. When Mrs Tunnisi finally notices Alyce on the ground, Annabelle is holding out her hand.

I can't believe Alyce is about to take it. With her IQ you'd think she'd know the meaning of dignity. I get there in time to help her myself.

'Get lost, Annabelle.' Alyce's knees are bloody. She's got a boot mark on her backside. Game over.

Corelli walks with us to the nurse. Every now and then he tries to catch her eye and smile. Alyce doesn't say a word.

By the time we come back for our bags everyone's gone except for Flemming. He's leaning against the change room wall, waiting for us. 'Are you okay?'

'A bit late to be asking now,' I snap. 'Don't you have friends to hang out with?'

'Gracie,' Alyce says after he's gone. 'He didn't pick me because I'm not good at basketball. This isn't his fault.'

'It's all their faults: Annabelle, Susan, Flemming, Belinda . . . What?' I ask, because she's staring at me, shaking her head.

'Nothing. I'll see you after recess. I'm going to wash up before class.'

'I'll come with you.'

'I'm better on my own.'

Alyce needs to tell Flemming to get lost if he's going to treat her like she's nothing. She won't tell him, though. She won't stop liking him. I've fed her chocolate. And now she knows how sweet it is she wants the whole block.

If you've never eaten chocolate before, though, eating the whole block can make you sick. Alyce sits in English after recess and quietly draws hearts on her page. Hearts. Alyce is strictly a squares and circles girl if she draws on her books at all. Most of the time she keeps every page neatly filled with the notes she takes in class. She's not even listening today.

'Alyce, what would you say is the main theme of the novel?' asks Mrs Wilson.

'Love,' she answers. At least she's right. And at least no one but me noticed that she hadn't even heard the question.

I get to practice early and wait for Flemming. As soon as he shows up I drag him around the corner. 'You should have picked Alyce today.'

'What?'

'For basketball. You let her stand there looking like an idiot.'

'Why would I pick her when she can't play?'

'Because she chose you to work with us on the English assignment last week when she knows you can't write to save yourself. You like her and you don't even have the guts to say it. Scared of people like Annabelle?'

'I'm not scared of anyone and that includes you.' He pushes past me.

'Ask Alyce to the dance, then.'

'What?'

'The dance next month. Ask her.'

'I don't want to ask her,' he says. There's a salty taste in my mouth. The taste of Alyce crying.

'Faltrain,' Flemming calls before I walk away. He looks around to check we're alone. 'Are you planning on telling Fuller what I said about her?'

'You think she doesn't know how you see her after what happened today? Alyce is the smart one, remember. It's you who's the idiot.' Flemming wants it both ways. But he can't kick Alyce in the teeth and expect her to smile about it.

Alyce isn't the only one who looks like she's been kicked in the teeth. Coach walks onto the field and tells us to do a warm-up jog. He spends the rest of the time watching us from the stands, calling out orders from there.

'He's freaking me out,' I say to Martin as we kick to each other. 'He hasn't said a word about Saturday.'

'It's coming,' Flemming says, overhearing me. 'I can feel it.'

At the end of practice Coach calls us all over. 'Sit down, everyone.' We wait for him to speak. He opens his mouth a few times before he starts.

'I know you want to win, and the other teams are rough, but you played wrong on Saturday. I taught you guys in Year 7 how to open up space in the goal square. You spread out and then pass.

'I still remember that goal Flemming kicked a minute before the whistle. It looked like we couldn't win. And then you all moved as if you had one mind. The whole team fanned out like a pack of cards and the opposition followed. It was beautiful. You remember that, Flemming?'

'I remember. But Coach, we're still working together.'

Coach's face dives a deeper shade of red. 'You're not playing like you've got one mind. You're playing like you've got one brain. There's a huge difference,' he shouts. 'Faltrain, you of all people should know what I'm talking about. You didn't beg to be on the team in Year 7 to play like this. Every kick you made last Saturday was weak. No way will a scout look twice at you, playing like that.' His words ache like a punch.

'For the rest of the week we'll work on tactics. But we don't play like that again.' He casts his eyes over every one of us. 'Promise me.'

We all make some sort of sign at him. Only Martin nods clearly. Coach drops his arms, like he's been carrying something too heavy, and walks off.

'He's right,' Martin says. 'You all know it.'

'We're allowed to play to win. Coach understands that, only he can't say it because he's a teacher.' The air is thick and heavy; it slows down Flemming's words and makes them hover longer than usual.

'You heard him. Scouts won't look twice at us if we don't show them what we can do,' I say.

'She's right,' Francavilla agrees.

'You think they'll look twice at us if we're knocked out in the first half?' Flemming asks. 'Yeah, Faltrain, you're not kicking the best goals of your life. But you're kicking.'

'So, what, we lie to Coach?' I ask. 'He's not an idiot. He watches the games.'

Flemming shrugs. 'He can't do much from the sidelines once the match has started.'

No one says yes. And no one says no. We're at the end of the day but it's not night yet. 'Can't see a thing,' Mum always says when she's driving at this time. 'Sun's gone. But the moon's not bright enough to shed any light on the road.'

'Who are you all?' Martin asks. But he doesn't wait for an answer.

There's an envelope on the hall table when I get home. It has my name on it, and the newspaper's address in the corner. I tip five letters onto my bed. All from women claiming to be Mrs Knight. All claiming to love their son, Martin.

'Gracie?' Mum knocks on my door. 'Is anything wrong? You didn't come and say hello.'

'I had a long practice, that's all.' I move my body over the letters. 'I'm starving though. I'll be down in a minute.'

'I saw that the paper sent you something.' I can tell she's been thinking about this since she got home. If forensics lifted prints from the envelope, Mum's would be all over it. She's been shaking it and holding it to the light like it's a Christmas present.

'You didn't do anything stupid, did you, Gracie?'

'Like what?'

'Like try to contact Mrs Knight?'

Part of me wants to tell Mum the truth. Coach was right today. I've changed. I'm playing a different game. But sometimes you don't have a choice, like Flemming said. If I lie down like Martin and Alyce, then who looks after them? Who looks after me?

'It's just a follow-up letter about the Firsts.'

Mum knows I'm lying, but she can't say it. The only proof is the letters and I've already pushed them behind me on the bed.

'Be careful, Gracie,' she says softly, and closes the door.

I read all the letters before I go to sleep. I look for clues in them, but I've never met Mrs Knight, so how can I tell if she's one of the writers? *I love you, son*, one letter finishes. *It's been too long*, another one starts. *I can't live without you anymore*, a third one adds as a PS.

Dear Marty, the last one starts, *by now you must be in Year 12. I guess it seems like the world will end if you fail, but just remember it's not whether you win or lose the game that matters, it's how you play.*

'It's her,' I whisper. I'd bet my life on it. I don't need to have met her to know. I've met her son.

I have to find a way to tell Martin the news about the letter without him spontaneously combusting. I have to find a way to convince him that this is the right thing.

Lying is a tricky business. Start with one and the whole thing snowballs. Pretty soon you're rolling down to the bottom of a hill in a huge ball of ice. And that's deadly. Just ask the person at the bottom.

Technically I haven't lied to Martin yet; I just didn't tell him I was putting the ad in the paper. 'That's a fine line, Faltrain,' Jane would say to me. But it's fine enough to see, and that's what counts.

Anyway, who cares what you think, Jane? You've made it pretty clear that you don't want me around anymore. This is my decision. I'm on my own.

30

'We're the only team everyone hates.
What does that tell you, Faltrain?' I ask.
'It tells me we're better than
everyone else, Martin,' she answers.
'Faltrain, they should measure your
head for science. I reckon it's the
biggest I've ever seen.'
Martin Knight

'Stop telling me what to do, Martin,' I yell during warm-up on Saturday. 'You're in goal, not on the field. You don't know what it's like.'

'I know you're better than this. It's embarrassing watching you out there.'

'Embarrassing?'

'I used to love seeing you play. I remember once, you were blocked in on all sides, and you spun around and did an overhead kick. It was absolutely amazing.'

'You're still going on about that boy I took down, aren't you? I've told you a million times, I couldn't have made it any other way. I would have missed. We would have lost.'

'So? Who cares? The old Faltrain didn't even know the meaning of the word missed.'

'Well the guy next to me in hospital explained it, you idiot. And he threw in a few more words, too, like humiliation and loser.'

Part of why I'm angry at Martin is because I know he's right. I'm not playing like I was before. None of us are. But we can't. The Firsts is a whole different game. With no space for risks.

We win the toss. Coach signals for us to take our positions. I don't feel excited like I usually do. I haven't felt that in weeks.

Coach calls time about twenty minutes into the first half. He's a walking heart attack. 'What are you playing at? It's a bloodbath out there, and you're all splashing around. You,' he turns to Flemming. 'The next time you aim for some guy's head and not the ball, I'm aiming for you. That goes for everyone.'

I'm learning a few lessons about human nature today. Lesson one? People have a survival instinct hard-wired into their brain. It takes over at the first hint of attack. Sometimes it takes over before. There's no space for sympathy out here. That path leads to the bench, or worse, hospital. There's only room for three things: run, hit, win. And, sometimes, duck.

Francavilla soars past number nine from the opposition, arms half out. He runs like a chicken all the time now, his elbows bent into bony wings, ready to belt anything in his flight path. He keeps them at the perfect height: not high enough to get red-carded but high enough to hurt. Number nine stumbles like he's drunk but keeps running.

No one sees that hit, though, because everyone's looking at Corelli. A striker from the opposition is trying to rip him apart at the shoulders. Corelli's discovered a new talent. His neck can spin almost three hundred and sixty degrees. 'My head's double-jointed,' he says, and then he passes out on his face.

'I hope his nose is double-jointed as well,' Flemming says,

watching him fall. After Corelli gets carried off, we play on, harder than before.

Flemming walks away at half time, so he's not there for Coach's speech. It's a good thing. His voice is so loud it dints my skin. 'Where the hell's Flemming?' he says, angry spit flying from his mouth. 'Find him, Faltrain. I want to talk to him before he goes back on and kills someone.'

I see him behind the change rooms, slamming his fist close to number seven's face, the guy who took Corelli out. Flemming stops short of punching him. A fight like that would lose him his place on the team, and he's too smart for that. He's out to scare. Or get revenge. Or both. 'You try that again and I'll find you,' he's saying. His face is twisted like a fist.

When the game's moving, it's easy not to think about what you're doing, I guess. A push here. A kick there. Everything gets lost in the rush, in the noise. It feels right because the ball goes into the goal. But there's no crowd around Flemming today. There's nothing for him to hide behind. It's one moment, picked out from all the rest. And it's wrong.

I wonder what my moment would have looked like, picked out from all the rest, slamming that guy in the balls to make the goal. If it were just him and me on the field alone, if I wasn't hidden in the crowd, I would have looked exactly like Flemming. I don't want him to catch me looking. I leave without making a noise.

'I don't know where Flemming is, Coach.' And I don't. There's no one back there that I recognise.

'You're doing well, Faltrain,' Flemming says when he re-appears on the field. 'Keep playing to win.' Number seven walks past us. There's the smallest bit of blood on his cheek.

I nod my head towards him. 'What happened to their striker?'

'No idea.' Flemming's playing a dangerous game. What's to stop that guy telling the ref? If the truth comes out Flemming'll be off the field for the rest of the season.

I can't help thinking that there's a whole team of us out here. And only Martin playing soccer. I don't look at Coach or Martin when I walk off at the end. I keep thinking about Flemming's face. And wondering if it looks like mine.

Martin, Flemming and Alyce come back to my place to celebrate. 'Did you see the way we thrashed them,' Flemming keeps yelling on the way home. His voice is too loud for Saturday afternoon. It belongs in the game.

'We were there. We saw it,' Martin says. He only puts up with Flemming these days because he knows that Alyce likes him.

We have a break after the first DVD. Martin and I stand outside. 'Be careful, Faltrain,' he says when we're alone.

'I can handle myself.'

He shakes his head. 'I didn't mean that. Mum told me once that you become who you set out to be.'

'So I'm setting out to win.'

'Does it feel like we're winning?'

Sort of. Maybe. I mean, I'm not in hospital after every game. I'm alive. Dad told me once that life's not black and white. It's blurred at the edges. So Flemming threatened a guy in the break. That guy hurt Corelli.

'Do you really think we should let them run all over us, knock us down, Martin? Is that how you want me to play the next game?' Half of me wants him to make it easy, give me the answers like he always does.

'The old Faltrain would never have played like this, that's all. She'd have found another way.'

'There is no other way. I'm not good enough. I'm not strong enough.'

'Then maybe the answer is that we walk.'

'Quit? Flemming would never agree to that.'

'I didn't ask *him* to walk.'

'You said you knew I'd always vote to fight. You told me that before we started playing like this.'

'Fight, fair enough. But not dirty. Not for the fun of it.'

'You think I'm having fun out there?'

'I think you're having the time of your life.' He's looking at me the way I looked at Flemming today. Like I'm ugly.

'Last year I would have trusted you with anything, Faltrain. And now I watch you play and you're like a stranger.'

It feels as though Martin's edging his way to a place I don't want to go, like he's about to tell me we're over. 'I'm the same person I always was,' I say.

'Are you?'

'Yes.' I say it louder so he believes it. I say it that way so I do, too. I try not to think about the ad and the letter and his mum. Martin has a way of reading my mind and the way he's talking tonight, I have a feeling that if he finds out what I've done, I'm dead. I have to change the subject. Quick. After a few minutes goldfish Martin will swim in and I'll be safe.

'What do you think Alyce and Flemming are talking about in there?'

Martin shrugs.

'Flemming's laughing. That's a good sign, right?'

'You and your stupid signs. You want to know how he really feels?' He picks up the soccer ball lying on the ground and launches it at the window. It smacks against the glass so loud Mum yells from the front room, 'Gracie Faltrain! Stop playing near the house.' I guess I've got my answer. Alyce and Flemming don't even look up. They just keep right on talking.

'He wants to walk me home,' Alyce whispers quickly when Flemming is out of the room. I should be happy for her. You take a chance and deal with whatever happens later. And if you don't take chances then you may as well be dead, right? But seeing Alyce happy makes me scared. Because the way Flemming's playing the game lately, I'm pretty sure she's not going to win.

When they walk off down the street, they're two shadows almost holding hands. That's meant to be the most exciting bit, the almost part, when nothing's happened but you're hoping it might. For the first time in my life, though, I think it might be better not to play. I can't bear to watch Alyce almost win the game she's been waiting to be picked for almost all of her life.

31

One bad pizza and you're vomit boy for
the rest of your life.
Freddy Jabusi

'Alyce,' I say, pulling the doona over my head. 'It's eight o'clock in the morning.'

'I'm just so excited.'

'Why?' I push the covers off my face so I can see her. 'He asked you to the dance after you left last night, didn't he?'

'Yes,' she squeals. 'Yes, yes, yes, yes!' Alyce looks like she has swallowed the sun. Not the hot and burning, middle-of-the-day sun, just the warm, end of afternoon one. I think I can actually see pink shining from her edges.

'So Alyce Fuller is about to score.'

Her eyes practically explode. 'Oh no . . .'

'Calm down. We'll get to that part later.' What was I thinking? Alyce has to crawl before she can walk.

'I think maybe he does like me, Gracie. Can you believe that?'

'Of course I can.' Good for you, Flemming. So you're not the biggest idiot of all time. 'We need to get you a killer dress, so you look hot at the dance.'

'I was thinking about something pink with long sleeves.'

I drag myself out of bed. Even on Sunday, my work is never done.

Jane and I always talked about what we'd wear to the Year 11 dance. 'You'll go with Nick,' she said. 'And I'll go with some mysterious guy from another school. We'll stay the night at your place and get ready together.'

It just goes to show that no one can predict the future.

'So I can't wait to see Annabelle's face when you tell her Flemming's your date,' I say to Alyce while we're looking at dresses.

'You can't tell her, Gracie.'

'Why?'

'Andrew asked me not to say anything. He wants some time to break the news to people.'

Sure he does. He wants, like, two years, until you're not in high school.

'I can't believe that idiot. He wants you to lie? What, does he expect you to wear a bag over your head so Annabelle doesn't know you're his date?'

'He's going to tell people, Gracie, when the time is right.'

The time would be right, right away. But if Flemming can't see that then we'll just have to show him. 'What about this one?' I pull a long black dress off the rack.

'I don't know, Gracie, it's a bit . . . revealing.'

'Just go and try it on, Grandma.'

Alyce comes out of the change room slowly, checking to see there's no one in the shop but me.

'Wow. You look fantastic. You've got boobs.'

She tries to stretch the top higher.

'Don't touch it. You look perfect.'

'I won't be comfortable.'

'It's the price you pay for fashion. Buy it.'

'He's taller than me.' She leans in to whisper. 'He'll see right down my top.'

Exactly. 'No he won't. Stop worrying so much.' And of course, as soon as I say that, in walks a reason to worry.

'Well, Alyce, buying a dress for the dance? It's so brave of you to go on your own.'

Annabelle: one. Opposition: zero.

'Alyce has a date, actually,' I answer.

One all.

'That's right. I did hear that Freddy Jabusi was looking for a partner.'

Let me explain just how nasty Annabelle is being here. Freddy Jabusi took Anita Fleck to a dance in Year 7. He was so nervous he vomited on her dress. In front of everyone. He'd had pizza for dinner. Annabelle Orion is suggesting that my best friend, Alyce Fuller, go to the dance with pizza vomit boy.

Annabelle: two. Gracie: one. But not for long.

'Alyce is going with Andrew Flemming. Susan must be so disappointed.'

Two all.

'Alyce and Flemming?' She starts to laugh. 'No way.' I can feel the advantage slipping away. Annabelle isn't upset. She's ecstatic. I've given her the best piece of gossip she's had all year.

It's not me who lost, though. It's Alyce. Up until I saw her face, white next to Annabelle's smile, I'd completely forgotten she was playing. Alyce hangs the dress back up as Susan walks in. Annabelle is going to love spreading this news.

'I'm sorry,' I say when we're sitting at the bus stop. 'But she would have found out sooner or later.' Alyce doesn't answer. The sun has disappeared from her face.

'Don't worry. People like Annabelle always get what they deserve.' I watch them walk out of the shop as the bus appears in the distance.

'Susan was crying,' Alyce says on the way home.

'What?'

'When they left the shop, Susan's eyes were all red.'

'Good. I hope she bawled her eyes out when Annabelle told her about you and Flemming.'

Alyce looks at me. 'What's the difference between her and me, Gracie?'

'You want the obvious answer?'

'No, really. She must have been so disappointed. She'll have to tell her mum that Andrew is going to the dance with someone else.'

'So, you're saying Flemming is the bad guy?'

'Sometimes there's not a bad guy, Gracie. Sometimes there's just another side.'

32

I'm a dog?
Alyce Fuller

'Heard you're taking Fuller to the dance,' Jason Newman says in the tuckshop line on Monday.

'So?' Flemming asks.

'So look at her, she's a dog.'

'Come on now,' Annabelle says, and for a second I think she's had a heart transplant. 'Even dogs don't have hair that bad.'

This is about the tenth time today I've heard some idiot make a comment about Alyce. Who do they think they are, the love gurus? If Flemming wants Alyce instead of Susan then it's none of anyone's business.

'I think she's cute,' says Corelli.

'Yeah, well, coming from the guy who had his head re-adjusted on the weekend, that doesn't mean much,' Jason laughs.

'Shut up, Newman.' Flemming should have been the one to say that, not Martin. But the second Flemming bought his sausage roll he ran.

'Good one, Martin,' I say.

'There's nothing good about this, Faltrain.'

He's right. Even I can see that Alyce has lost the game. Now we just have to get her off before she breaks something –

'I give it two more days,' Annabelle says to Susan.

– like, say, her heart.

33

Running an ad in the paper once:
forty-five dollars.
Running it twice: ninety dollars.
A warning that the bill's arrived and your
parents are about to kill you? Priceless.
Gracie Faltrain

'Gracie,' Mum calls out from the kitchen when I walk in the door after school. 'Your dad and I would like to talk to you.' When both parents want to talk it can only mean one thing: interrogation.

'What is it?'

'My MasterCard statement arrived today.'

I think I need a lawyer.

'It seems that someone other than me has been using my account.'

A really good lawyer.

Mum and Dad sit across the table from me. I'm surprised she doesn't drag the lamp over and shine it in my face.

'Where were you on the night of the third?'

I shift around in my seat. 'Home.'

'I know you were home, Gracie Faltrain,' her voice gets louder. 'Because I have the statement to prove it.' She pulls it out from under the table. The woman watches more television than me. 'You put an ad in the paper to find Martin's mother. You stole my credit card.'

'Stole's a strong word.'

'I'm sorry. You took my credit card and used it without asking. Is that better?'

'I had to do it for Martin.'

'Why didn't you use his dad's money? Or at least ask me first?'

The room feels hot. My jumper is itchy. Mum won't stop staring.

'Martin doesn't know, does he? *Does he*?' Her last words grab me by the shoulders and shake me.

'No.'

'Gracie, what have you done? People's lives aren't something to mess around with. That family is hurting. This could hurt them even more.'

'I'm fixing things for them.'

'You're fixing things the way you always do, by running and breaking them. This isn't a game of soccer. This is life.'

'I know that.'

'You don't, Gracie. You're a kid. How could you know what that family's going through?'

'You think I don't know what it's like to miss having your family together? I was here last year, remember, when Dad was away. The only thing I wanted was for him to come back. I would have done anything to make that happen.'

'Gracie, this isn't the same thing. Martin's mum walked out for good. She left that family with no explanation and Clem Knight had to stay behind to pick up the pieces.'

'Well he didn't do a very good job, did he?' I yell.

'I'd say he did a bloody fantastic job, a damn sight better than your father and I. Haven't we taught you anything?'

Her last words suck the air out of me. Her face is the colour of ash after fire, white but hot.

'I think you should go to your room, Gracie,' Dad says.

I sit on my bed and stare at the floor. I don't get changed, or turn on music. My legs ache from Saturday's game. My throat hurts from yelling. My chest hurts most of all. Because that's where Mum's words are sitting.

She creeps into my room at six this morning. I know the time because I'm wide awake. She gets under the covers with me and lies there the way she did when I was a kid.

'Gracie, I'm sorry.' Her voice is like my legs after soccer, shaky and tired. 'But you're changing people's lives in a way that you can never undo.'

It's too hot under the doona. My head feels full of rain. Last week everything seemed clear. Martin would always be in the goal square unless he found his mum. Flemming was right about the way we should play. I'm not sure about anything anymore.

'So I won't tell him. I'll throw the letter out. Martin will never have to know.'

'There's a woman on the other end of that letter, Gracie.'

'She walked out. She's the one who hurt him.'

'So she deserves to have her hopes raised and then dropped? She's his mother. He's her blood. I've always tried to let you make your own mistakes. And most of the time you find your way. But you have to step into Martin's life and imagine what he's going through.'

'I did.'

'No, you put Martin's life on over your own. You imagined how he would feel if he was you. You got it all backwards.'

'So how can I fix things?'

'You have to go forwards now, Gracie. You have to play this out to the end.'

'But if I tell Martin I'll lose him.' I'm sure of it, after Saturday night.

'I know and I'm sorry,' Mum says. 'But it's time for you to hear the hard stuff. You have to lose this time. There's just no other way you can win.'

34

Okay. *Now* I get it.
Gracie Faltrain

I have this feeling in my stomach all week like I'm walking along a shaky bridge overhanging a very deep ocean. The letter from Mrs Knight is as heavy as a hundred bricks in my bag. I've been carrying it with me everywhere along with the ad, trying to find a way to explain to Martin what I've done without losing him.

'Faltrain, is there something wrong?' he asks while we're sitting in the café after school, waiting for our drinks to arrive.

'No, why?'

'You've been acting weird all week.'

'No I haven't.'

'Are you worried about the match this Saturday?'

'A bit, I guess. It's rougher now that we're close to the final. It's not easy playing when there's a team out to get me.'

'There's always someone out to get you, Faltrain. Last year it was your own team. Is winning so important that you'd give up the whole reason you love the game? It's not about playing rough; it's about skill. That's what you always said to me.'

'There's no way out now, Martin.'

'There's always a way. Like my mum said, "Marty, it's not whether you win or lose the game that matters" . . .'

'I have to go to the bathroom.' I can't listen to him talking about playing fair anymore. Not when I've been rolling around in the mud for weeks.

I make a decision while I'm in the bathroom. I love Martin. I want him to trust me again. I can't lose him. And I won't. Mum's wrong; I can start playing a different game from now on. It's not too late.

When I get back, Martin's holding my bag, staring at me. The afternoon has disappeared from his eyes.

'I forgot my wallet,' he says. 'I used yours.'

'That's fine. Are you okay?'

'You're a crap liar, Faltrain. I knew something was up.' It's only then that I see the letter and the ad, crumpled in his hands, as well as my bag. 'I recognised her handwriting straight away.'

'Martin, let me explain . . .'

'I don't want to hear it.' He clenches his teeth. He sounds like he's drowning, his words gurgling up from somewhere way down inside of him. Before, when Martin tried to explain about his mum, it was just words. Today I see his eyes filling up, ready to spill. I see the inside of him, the things he's been hiding. I see years and years of hurt.

'I don't even know you anymore. You cheat on the field, you lie to me. You treat Alyce like dirt . . .'

'What?'

'Gracie Faltrain is only interested in helping one person. Herself.'

His feet tap out a fast beat on the concrete as he runs away. My heart taps out a slow sad one. And they don't match at all.

'Gracie, why do you live like this?' Mum asks.

Because I'm stupid. Because I never see anything until it's right up in my face, and by then it's too late. I need life glasses, to blow everything up to three times the size so I can see things coming.

'I've lost him, haven't I?'

Love's like an egg. Break it, and you might still have almost every bit of yolk and white, but there's no way you're getting that back in the shell. And even if you could, there'd still be all the cracks. It's why Mum and Dad are taking all winter to grow the smallest bit of green. It's why Mrs Knight never came back.

'Yes, Gracie, love.' Mum doesn't bother lying. 'I think you've lost him for now.'

35

Scientific tests have recently proven that goldfish can actually remember for up to three months. They can also be taught to follow a routine and tell the time.
Alyce Fuller, science report, Year 7

Martin ignores me for the rest of the week. He sees me waiting in the canteen line and walks straight past. No smile. No get me a Coke, Faltrain. No nothing. There's a hole in the day without him. Every bone in my body is heavy, like when I had the flu. Only I know that this flu is going to last a long time. As long as Martin's gone.

'Did you two have a fight?' Alyce asks when he walks past me in the line. I can't bring myself to tell her what I've done.

'Yeah. But you know Martin, he's like a goldfish. He'll forget by the weekend.' Please let him forget. I look at Alyce and silently beg her to agree with me, so I don't feel so bad.

'Actually, goldfish have very good memories,' Alyce says.

Perfect. Now she tells me.

36

I find her sitting in a classroom on Friday
and I just tell her straight away. I say,
'I made a mistake asking you to
the dance'. I say, 'Fuller, we don't even have
anything in common. All you do is read.'
And she looks at me and says, 'It's okay,
Andrew'. I mean, who the hell tells the guy
who dumps her that it's okay?
Andrew Flemming

'Hey, Flemming,' I call out when I see him leaving after school. 'Wait up. You want to go to a movie this afternoon?'

'Can't, Faltrain. My dad's picking me up. I'm suspended for the rest of the day.'

'Not from soccer as well?'

He shakes his head.

That's a relief. 'What did you do?'

'I threw a chair at a classroom window. Don't look so worried. I missed.'

'Why'd you do it?'

'Because I felt like it, Faltrain. I just felt like it. End of story. Why don't you go with Alyce?'

'She went home sick.'

'Maybe you should check on her, then.' His dad pulls up and he gets in the car and slams the door without saying goodbye.

I go to the movies on my own. I tell Mum I'm with Alyce so she won't worry about me. I sit up the back and enjoy the darkness until Dan Woodbury walks in with his mates and sits in the row in front. There's no way out. I have to listen to him going on and on about how he kicked the best goal of his life last week.

'We're playing Faltrain's team tomorrow,' his mate says.

'Don't worry, Moko. She shouldn't be hard to beat. She plays like a girl.'

For the second time this month I leave before the film starts. I'm so happy I bought a Coke instead of chips. 'Take that, Woodbury,' I say, pouring the drink over his head, spraying his mates at the same time. 'You idiot.'

37

You want to play it like that, Faltrain, then
let's play. We'll see how you like it.
Martin Knight

I test Alyce's theory at the match today. Martin seems to have developed a rock-solid memory. 'Get lost, Faltrain,' he says before I even open my mouth. And then he turns his back.

I used to think that what I loved about soccer was that it was simple. I could do it. I could win. But I'm learning that there are other things that are great about it, and one of them is Martin laughing, shaking his head from side to side at me, saying stuff like, 'Remind me never to get in your way, Faltrain'. He's the best thing about soccer. I just never realised it.

I have to show Martin today that I'm the old Gracie. We have to play like before.

'Flemming!' I run over to him in warm-up. 'We need to talk.'

'You heard, then?'

'Heard what?' But I know what he's about to say before he answers. Call it sixth sense. Call it intuition. Actually, let's just call it what it is: freaking bad luck.

‘Let me guess, you’re about to say that the guy over there who looks like a tank wants to teach me a lesson and has trained every gorilla on his team to attack at the sound of my voice?’

‘Knight told you about Michael Moko, huh?’

‘No. I poured a can of Coke over his head at the movies last night.’

The important thing is to remain calm. Say after me: I am not scared of Michael Moko. I am not scared of Michael Moko. So he’s six-foot-three with a team of mutant gorillas ready to do whatever he tells them. So he wants me dead. I can handle that.

And usually I could. But usually I have Martin.

I look into the crowd for Mum and Dad. There’s an empty seat next to them. I wish Alyce wasn’t sick. I need all the support I can get.

‘The team has your back, Faltrain,’ Flemming says, and runs to the centre. Not the whole team, Flemming. Martin ignores me on his way past to goal. ‘Any last words of advice?’ I call to him. Please give me one tiny sign that you only hate me, not want me completely smashed into the ground. He shakes his head.

And the game begins.

It becomes pretty clear from the minute the whistle goes that I’m more than just in the soccer game. I am the game. Gracie Faltrain, forget playing dirty, get the hell out of the way.

Moko is out to get me. I feel his breath against my neck, scratching at me like a jumper that’s too tight. Flemming runs in, arms out, and elbows him on the way past. Moko doesn’t go down. He gets madder. He waits until I have the ball and then he slams into the side of me. It feels like I’ve hit concrete, not grass. I get up and spit blood. I check all my teeth are where they should be.

Ref calls time. Coach runs over to him. I can see them shaking their heads.

'He said it looked like an accident, Faltrain.' Coach wipes my face while I sit on the sidelines. 'I didn't see it. But it's safe to say that there's a team out there that wants you dead.'

'Really? I hadn't noticed.'

'I think you should sit the rest of this one out.'

'No way. You need me in there.'

'I need you alive.' He looks back onto the field, where Singh and Francavilla are racing for the ball. The opposition are racing too. Corelli gets in the way and there's a head-on collision with all five of them. Coach closes his eyes. 'It's not soccer, Faltrain, playing like this.'

'When the game's this rough, how else can you win?'

He looks at me and takes a final check of my face. 'You guys could beat every team from here on in, and you still won't win. Now get out there. And be careful.'

Easier said than done, Coach. When I fall down for the third time, I know I won't make it up again. I lie there, on my back, every muscle aching. The ref calls time. Dad calls, 'Gracie!' I'm thinking, isn't somebody calling for an ambulance? 'It's over,' I say, and wait to be carried off.

'Your back broken?' Martin asks, standing over me.

'No.'

'Any other bones?'

'I don't think so.'

'Then it's not over. Get up.' He heaves at my arm. 'You wanted to play like this, Faltrain. You wanted to get dirty with the rest of them, so finish what you started.' He pushes me back into play. He runs over to goal. And stands there watching while I get pummelled.

And believe me, I get pummelled. I am dough by the sixty-minute mark. I am ready to be rolled out and put in the oven. But the thing that hurts more than the knocks? The thing that hurts even more than the humiliation? Is that Martin doesn't once try to help.

In the last five minutes of the game the opposition are one goal ahead. Moko takes possession of the ball. I need to make this shot. I need to leave the game with some respect. I chase him. I chase him hard. I get the ball to Flemming before Moko shoves me in the ribs and I'm out for the count.

Flemming picks up where I fell off and runs with it. If he scores then we tie the game. I can see why Alyce likes him, today. There's almost zero chance that he can make it but he doesn't care about the odds. He swerves around Moko and misses being tripped by a beat. There's no doubt in my mind that in the final stretch, the ball belongs to him. He kicks and scores on the whistle. We tie. By a breath. But it's getting harder and harder to win.

'Martin, wait!' I call after the match.

'Faltrain, I don't want to talk to you.'

'Martin, please. I'm sorry.'

'Sorry isn't enough this time. You can't fix this.'

'I can try.'

'You can try?' he says, his voice scraping out from his throat. 'You have no idea what it's like for me, for anyone other than yourself. Everything is about you, what you want.' Martin raising his voice is like snow falling in summer. It's wrong.

'I've never told you about what it was like for me that day, have I? What it was like knowing that my mum kissed me goodbye in the morning, quicker than usual, because she was waiting to run the minute I was out of sight? She didn't care about Karen and me then, and she doesn't now.'

'Martin, she loves you, I know it.' I've cut him and I need to get close enough to stop the blood.

'You don't know anything. You don't leave the people you love. You just don't.' He wipes his nose against the back of his sleeve. 'You think I need to hear her say that? There was a note, Faltrain. She left a note.'

'But you said you'd never read it.'

'I asked Dad for it when I came back from the Championships. The paper was thin, like he'd read it a million times. I sat on the bed for ages, just holding it in my hands, holding the last piece of her.'

'What did it say?'

'It said, "Goodbye, Clem". It didn't even mention me. I'd spent years imagining how hard it was for her to leave me and Karen. I'd read that note a million times in my head. And in the end I wasn't even in it.'

So that was it. The secret Martin had been holding on to. It was so small. And so awful. I don't even have to try, now. I can see the world through Martin's eyes. Not how I imagine things would look, but how they are. The world is too bright, like I've been asleep for days and finally blinked my eyes open in glaring sun. It hurts to see in this light. It burns. Martin loving his mum as much as I love mine and walking into a house empty of her. Martin holding that letter, her last thoughts before she stepped out the door. And he wasn't in them.

My head is pounding from the game; a bruise is thumping

out over my left eye. I kneel down and take deep breaths, but nothing works. I'm sick on the grass.

Martin doesn't hold my hair back or ask if I'm all right. He waits for me to finish. 'I told you, Faltrain,' he says, his voice as empty as the middle of the night. 'I told you what would happen if you weren't careful with my family. And you hammered into us without a thought.'

'No, Martin, I did it because I cared.'

'Can't you see? Other people have a right to decide things for themselves. What would have happened if she'd walked in on Dad and Karen? My whole family, everything that I've fought for since she left, would have been back to square one.'

'Martin, I'm so, so sorry.'

'Just leave me alone.'

'You're not taking me to the dance?' Even as I say it I know how dumb it sounds. But I want things to be like they were three days ago. I want to somehow remind Martin of what we were before this.

'You promised you wouldn't try to find my mum. You lied to me, Faltrain. *All year*. Why would I take you anywhere?'

Martin's not in the quiet anymore. He's in the middle of a twisting storm. The thing is, that storm was always going to shift, and I guess Martin knew that. It's why he was buried so far under the ground, waiting for it to pass. But I dug him out and pushed him into the open. Good one, Gracie Faltrain, I think, as the wind picks him up. And tosses him far away.

I can't decide what to do after Martin goes. I lie down on the ground and stare at the sky slowly turning to black. My feet take me to Alyce's house in the end.

The light is on in her bedroom, so I knock on her window.

'Gracie?' She pulls the curtain across. 'What is it?'

'Can I come in?'

'I'm sick. Is it important?'

She comes to the front of the house and lets me in. There's an edge to her voice that I've never heard before. It's hard, like a straw broom sweeping away the mess on the path.

'Alyce, Martin won't talk to me.'

The one thing I can count on is that Alyce will be on my side. I spill out my story to her; I need her to tell me I'm not as bad as Martin says I am.

'Gracie, you did a terrible thing. He trusted you.'

'But I was trying to help.' Even I can hear that I sound like a broken record.

'You never think before you do things.' She's not yelling. Alyce hardly ever raises her voice, even when she's excited. It's light, like a giant balloon floating, tonight, with fire flashing every now and then. 'Can't you see that pushing me and Flemming together and telling Annabelle about the dance is just like Martin helping you in the tryouts?'

Well, when you put it like that. 'But my plan worked. You're Flemming's date.' I don't say it with all that much fire. If I was a balloon I'd be plummeting towards the earth right about now.

'Just because you think it worked doesn't make it right. If you make my life like yours, it's not mine anymore.'

'But all I wanted was for you to be happy.'

'You never even asked me if I was unhappy. You just assumed I must be because I'm Alyce Fuller.'

'But being with Flemming makes you happier, right?' I need to know that I haven't completely stuffed up another person's life.

'He took it back. He's going to the dance with Susan.'

'But he can't do that.'

'Why, because they're not Gracie Faltrain's rules? He can do whatever he likes. I can't make him take me.'

'I can't believe you let him walk all over you. Don't you get sick of people treating you like that, Alyce?'

'Yes,' she says quietly, and stops pacing. She looks at me for a long time. I need to get away from those eyes. I need to run and kick goals. I need to be the old me.

'You tell me what to do all the time. You push me around. You give my secrets to Annabelle. You sign me up for debates without asking.'

'They chose you for the team? That's fantastic, Alyce.'

'I told you I didn't want to do it.'

'You'll be great, though. I'm sure of it.'

'You don't have to convince me. You're the one who thinks I have to prove myself.'

'If people don't see who you really are, Alyce, they'll always treat you like dirt.'

'I know,' she says, and opens her bedroom door for me to leave. 'Gracie, can't you see who you really are? You're Annabelle. You're just on my side.'

'Duck, Faltrain,' I imagine Jane saying, 'there's that unexpected cow coming your way.'

38

Can't find Gracie Faltrain in
the dictionary? She's next to Alyce.
Try looking under L.
Annabelle Orion

People always say that things look brighter in the morning. But when I wake up on Sunday everything looks worse. It looks that way on Monday, too.

I'm starting to think that life is an escalator that keeps looping around and around the same way. Unless you grab on to something and haul yourself off, then things never change. But the crap thing is, you jump from a moving escalator and it's going to hurt. Big time.

'Life's about falling over and getting up again, Gracie,' Mum says this morning. 'I would have thought you'd know that better than anyone.'

'But I fell over last year.'

'What? You think because you have one thing go wrong nothing bad ever happens again? Sorry to disappoint you.'

'This is worse than last year, though. Martin looked at me like I was nothing on Saturday. He said I treat Alyce like dirt.'

'Do you treat her like that? Gracie?' She reaches across the table for my hand.

'I can see how it might seem that way, especially after what she said on Saturday,' I say.

'What did you do, Gracie?' Mum asks.

'I set her up with Flemming.'

'And?'

'He dumped her before the dance.'

'And?'

'I told Annabelle Orion some stuff that Alyce didn't want her to know.' Now I'm on a roll, I might as well confess to the lot. 'And that made Annabelle mad and she tripped Alyce over in sport.'

'Is that it?'

'I signed Alyce up for the comedy debate when she told me she didn't want to do it.'

Mum rubs her face with her hands. She can't even look at me. And that's when I know I'm in trouble.

I guess when you list all the things I've done like that, one after the other, it does look bad. But that's like reading the words to a song without listening to the music. You only get half the picture. 'I wanted to help Alyce, Mum. People are always calling her a nerd. I wanted her to know what it's like to have friends.'

'Alyce has friends, Gracie. At least she did. She had you and Martin for a start. All you did was prove to her that you don't think she's good enough the way she is. Is she good enough for you?'

I think about all the things Alyce has done for me. Talking to me last year when no one else would. Writing to the paper. Making me feel like I'm home. 'Too good.'

'Then stop worrying about what everyone else thinks. Stop trying to make her into another Jane.'

Good advice, Mum. Just a little too late to stop the Gracie Faltrain express. 'She won't talk to me anymore. She kicked me out of her house on Saturday.'

'I have a feeling Alyce is the sort of person who will let you fix things. So is Martin, eventually.'

'How do I fix things, though?'

'Gracie, haven't you learnt anything from your father?'

Don't read the last page of the book first? 'I don't know. What was I meant to learn?'

'He's been proving himself to us all year, working to get our trust again. Find a way to go back to who you were. The old Gracie Faltrain did things wrong, you fought to make the world how you wanted it to be, but you never lied. You never cheated.'

She stares out of the kitchen window. 'Some friends are so good they come back better than before when you test them, like lemons and oranges. They need a harsh frost to sweeten them up.' She turns to me. 'I can't tell you that Alyce and Martin will forgive you. But they're worth fighting for. It's not spring yet. Cut the garden back. And see what happens.'

I guess Mum means lose the crap bits of me and see what's left. Maybe if I flower like magnolia, Martin and Alyce will like me again.

It's unlikely. Alyce won't look at me today. She'll never believe I'll be anything but grey and bare. There's an empty desk next to her in maths, but she doesn't shift her books so I can sit down. It's wrong to be in a classroom and not talk to her. It feels like an episode of *The Twilight Zone*, where last year never happened. Martin and I never got together. Alyce and I never became friends.

'Heard you don't have a date for the dance anymore, Alyce,' Annabelle calls out from her seat at the back. 'Loser.'

Some things haven't changed. I open my mouth to shout something but I stop. This is Alyce's fight. It's Alyce's life. If she'd turn around and ask me to help I'd do anything. But that's the thing. She's never asked.

'Freddy,' Annabelle calls out as he walks in. 'Alyce needs a date for the dance.' The whole class laughs, except for four people: Freddy, Alyce, me, and Flemming. Everyone is looking at Flemming, wondering what he's going to do. I know he has been copping it from his mates ever since it got out that he liked the biggest nerd in the class. But that big nerd helped when you needed it, Flemming, I want to yell at him. Now save her.

But people always save themselves first. They make all those movies where the hero risks his life to find the kid in the burning house and carry him out, but how often does that actually happen? In the real world, it's so much easier to cut someone loose. It's easier to run. And afterwards you can tell yourself a whole bunch of lies so you don't feel bad.

I hate the thought of Alyce choking in her burning house, the flames shooting up against a sky bloody with heat. She turns back to look at Flemming. And he does what 99.95 per cent of the population would do.

'Go on, ask her, Freddy,' he says. And then under his breath, but loud enough for Annabelle's entire crowd to hear, 'Vomit boy.' Flemming stands on the footpath with the rest of the crowd and watches Alyce burn.

I know how I would have acted in Alyce's place. I would have slammed my books down and walked up to Flemming and done some detailed dentistry on his two front teeth. I'm the same person that I saw behind the change rooms, slamming my fist at the enemy.

I look around at the class, all calling out and cracking jokes. They're lighting every last match in their box and tossing them at the fire. Annabelle and Susan are toasting marshmallows, loving the sticky sweetness of Alyce's embarrassment. Flemming's face is a little too hot. He looks like he's about to run. This is the real world I wanted Alyce to live in. These are the people that I wanted her to fit in with.

The thing is, Alyce doesn't burn. She doesn't even singe. She moves her books so Freddy can sit next to her. She smiles at him. And while everyone's still laughing at the idea of her and vomit boy dancing together, she leans over and lends him her pen.

Martin's not on the field when I walk up to practice this afternoon. The rest of the team is crowded around Coach. 'Faltrain, I need to talk to you,' he says.

'What is it?'

'When did you last see Knight?'

'Saturday. Why?'

Coach puts his hand on my shoulder. 'His dad came to talk to me this morning. Martin didn't go home last night.'

The colour drains out of the afternoon until it's black. I practise like this. In the dark. Running into shadows.

'Faltrain, are you okay?' Flemming asks after practice.

I can't answer.

'You should go home, in case Knight calls.'

His hand on my shoulder is light and warm. It doesn't match with the person on the field who runs next to me, ripping heads and arms. It doesn't match with the person who dumped Alyce. He's like a mirror, smashed on the ground, reflecting different bits of sky.

If you put all those parts together, though, Flemming makes perfect sense. Everything he's done lately, in soccer, with Alyce, has all been for the same reason: he's scared of losing. He's scared of being beaten.

'Martin won't call,' I say. 'He's not coming back.'

'You don't know that, Faltrain.'

'Yes I do.'

There'll be a game on Saturday, and Martin won't play. I'll have to get up every morning and go to school and Martin won't be there to say, 'Faltrain, stop stuffing around, you'll be late for class.' I'll never see him again but he'll be the stupid voice in my head for the rest of my stupid life and I'll never be able to shut him up. And there's no one to blame but myself.

'How do you know? What happened?'

'I lied to him, about his mum. I tried to find her after I promised I wouldn't. I was too much of an idiot to see that he needed to forget her . . .' The words running out of my mouth barely make sense to me. 'And Alyce won't talk to me, either. I made her feel like crap because she's different. Just like you did.' The end of my sentence spins from my mouth like a knife and finishes with the point aimed at Flemming. 'How can you like Alyce as much as you do and hurt her?'

'I made a mistake asking her to the dance, that's all, like you did looking for Knight's mum. People make mistakes, Faltrain.'

Yeah. They do. Except what we did was deliberate. Martin told me a million times to stay out of it. He begged me. And I kept going. I kept pushing. He told me to stop playing dirty and I didn't care. I wanted to win. Just like Flemming. He knew what would happen if he asked Alyce to the dance. If he couldn't follow through he should have kept his stupid mouth shut.

'That's crap,' I say. 'Annabelle told you to take Susan.'

'You think I'd do something because Annabelle told me to?'

'I think you would if your mates agreed with her. Alyce is worth a hundred of Annabelle and her friends. She was the best thing that ever happened to you.' My voice is loud. It's full of everything I've done.

'Calm down, Faltrain.'

But I can't. It's all messed together, now. Me, what I did to Martin. Flemming and what he did to Alyce. 'I don't want to be calm. She trusted you and when it really counted, you let her down.' Just like I did to Martin.

'No one told me what to do.'

'You wanted to dump Alyce the week before the first dance she's ever been asked to?'

'I told you. I made a mistake asking her. I'm sorry.'

His voice is too close to mine. I can hear myself saying to Alyce and Martin over and over how sorry I am. But it doesn't mean anything. It doesn't fix anything.

'You deserve everything you get,' I say. We both do. I slam my fist into his face and clip the side of his mouth. I catch him off guard, and he stumbles backwards. He sits on the ground and wipes a red trickle from his lips. There's blood on my knuckle. I don't bother wiping it off.

'Get up,' I say.

'What?'

'Get up. Or don't you like it so much when you're the one getting hit?'

'You want to fight me?'

'Get up.'

'I'm not punching a girl.'

I kick his leg. Hard. 'Too scared to fight?' I kick him again, anger racing through me. This is what I am. This is how I solve things. This is what Martin saw in all of us. 'Hit me,' I yell, swinging my words around him. 'You're hopeless. You're hopeless at school and the only thing you can do is play soccer . . .'

The look on Flemming's face tells me I've found the other reason he won't go to the dance with Alyce. Annabelle is just the surface, the skin. The other reason is the blood of it. I cut way down deep to get to it. I don't care about the mess.

'You're too stupid for her. That's it, isn't it? She'll spend time with you and find out what an idiot you really are. You can't even think of what to say when you're with her . . .'

'Shut up, Faltrain,' he warns.

But I'm just warming up. It feels good to hurt Flemming like he hurt Alyce. And I want to get part of what I deserve for all the crap things I've done this season. 'She uses words you haven't even heard of.'

His face is closing in like it did that day behind the change rooms. 'I said shut up.'

'She probably did most of the assignments for you, didn't she? What'll you do now that you can't use her anymore? Cheat?'

There's a button in most people that turns them into someone else. It sends them spinning like a car, tyres blown on the freeway. Most people never know what they'll do when they hit that point, because they spend their lives staying away from it. Like Martin. Like Alyce.

Flemming hits that point now. He jumps up and grips the collar of my shirt, body knuckled with anger. Today I'm every person who's ever told him he's stupid, that he won't make it.

'You don't know anything, Faltrain,' he shouts. 'You don't know me.' He pulls his fist back and swings as hard as he can. I shift my head to the right just in time. His fist sings past my ear and he stumbles forwards onto the ground.

He sits up and blinks. He looks empty, like the person who was holding him up a second ago walked out, and he has to wait for the person who's taking over to arrive.

He meant to hit me. If I'd been a second slower he'd have broken my nose. We both know that. I can see now how easy it was for Flemming and me to end up where we are. And how easy it would have been to end up somewhere different.

'Are you okay?' he asks after a while.

'I'm fine.'

'You don't know me, Faltrain,' he says quietly, staring at his fists.

But I do. Because for the first time, I think I know myself.

Mum and Dad are sitting at the kitchen table when I get home, their hands locked together. 'Oh thank God,' Mum says. 'Were you with Martin?'

'No. Coach told me he's missing.'

'Mr Knight called. He's out of his mind with worry. Did Martin tell you where he was going?'

'No. Did you say anything about what I did, about the letter?'

'We had to, Gracie. The police need to know everything,' Mum answers.

'Was Mr Knight mad?'

'He's in shock, love. I said we'd take you over as soon as you came home, so you can tell him and the police what you know.'

Everything's unravelling tonight. I could tell you it's like a ball of wool or string, or something. But I think a better description would be to say that everything's unravelling like Gracie Faltrain's life. I'm back at the beginning of the end of the last season. Again.

There are more lights on in the house than I've ever seen before. It's like Mr Knight's worried that Martin will forget where he lives and need some reminding. 'Come in, love,' he says when he opens the door. He shakes Mum and Dad's hands and thanks them for coming.

Even though I've never met Mrs Knight, I always thought Martin was more like her than like his dad. I guess that was because Martin was always telling me stuff she'd said about soccer, about life, and he always seemed to be trying to do what she told him. All those things she said don't add up to much, though. 'Live like you play, Marty. Everyone's desperate for something. You become who you set out to be, Marty.' She left him with a whole life to live and a bunch of sayings to work out how to do it. Mr Knight did the rest.

He's polite to me and I don't understand why. If someone had forced Martin out of my life I'd be angry. I'd shout. Punch. Kick. They wouldn't deserve anything else. He takes my jacket and shows me into the lounge.

'Gracie, Bill, Helen, this is Constable Rick Blythe. Gracie is Martin's best friend.'

Was, I think as I nod at Mr Blythe.

'I was just saying, I can take down any information that you have, and circulate a description, but there's not a lot we can do. Martin's almost eighteen. All the evidence suggests that he has run away.' He flips open a notebook. 'Do you know what happened to Martin, Gracie?'

'No.'

'When did you last see him?'

'Saturday.'

'Did he say anything to you about where he might be going?'

'We weren't speaking. He was angry at me because . . .' I take a quick glance at Mr Knight. 'I tried to look for his mum and he didn't want me to.'

'Did you find her?'

'She sent a letter. At least I think it was her. Martin kept it.'

'Is it possible that he would try to make contact?'

'I don't think so. He was angry at me because he didn't want to have anything to do with her.'

'Still, it's worth checking. Did the letter have a number or an address?'

'It did, but I didn't keep a copy.'

'Maybe the paper . . .' Mr Knight says, his eyes hopeful.

'They won't have read the replies; just forwarded them on. We can try, though. I take it you don't have contact with your ex-wife, Mr Knight?'

'I haven't heard from her since the day she left. I have no idea how to find her.'

'I do,' Mum says. 'I read the letter, and took down the number.' She turns to me. 'Call it instinct, Gracie. I had a feeling you might need a little help.'

Call it instinct. Call it Helen Faltrain. Call it anything you like. Just call that woman.

Mr Knight puts his head in his hands after the policeman leaves. I don't say sorry, because it's such a tiny word and it won't be big enough to cover the hole I've made.

'I tried to find her, too, after she left,' he says after a while. 'Martin was still a kid. She didn't want to be found then, I guess.' There's not enough voice in him to make more than a whisper. I want him to get angry, to tell me I'm stupid, that it's my fault Martin's gone, so that everything is out in the open and I can feel better. But he doesn't.

I look around the lounge. The couch is new. The chairs are as well. I was with Martin when the family picked them out. I'd forgotten about that day until now. Karen looked like we were all going on a holiday when we got in the car. She was so happy, and I thought it was sad that something so small could make her that excited.

But I guess the couch and chairs were a sign that they were all together, and planning on staying that way for a while. A kind of promise from her dad. The rest of the place looks tired and old. It probably hasn't changed all that much since Mrs Knight left.

Karen must have felt so happy after the Championships because her dad started moving through the water, wading forwards. And then I come along and sink him and she loses it all again. For everyone's sake, I wish I could say something to hold Mr Knight's head above the current. I can see now that he only has the energy to float, and that Martin leaving will be too heavy for him.

'Anyone want a cup of tea?' I ask. They all nod, and I go into the kitchen for some air, some space from the things I've done. I'm dunking the last tea bag when I hear a chair pull out behind me. Karen is sitting, watching me, her head resting on her hands. Her eyes seem bigger today. Big enough to get lost in. 'Is he coming back, Gracie?' she asks.

I stop dunking. I know I should answer, but I can't, because I keep thinking about who she reminds me of, with those sad, wide eyes, and her small voice.

'Gracie?'

She's Martin. All those years ago. Before I knew him. And just like that I step right into his life, into this kitchen with the faded yellow paint on the walls and the table full of cuts and knocks. I imagine him coming home that day, staring at her apron, hanging on the back of the door, still smelling of her, still full of her shape. I see Martin, a kid like Karen, with his head resting in his hands. 'Is she coming home, Dad?'

'I don't know, Karen,' I say. 'I hope so.'

People's lives shouldn't loop like this. It's not fair. And I'm the one who set the escalator on go.

'You didn't make this mess,' Mr Knight says before we leave. 'It was here long before you arrived.' Maybe, but I made it worse. And somewhere Martin is hurting because of it.

'Why were you so late tonight?' Dad asks while we're driving home.

'I got into a fight. With Andrew Flemming.'

'A fight?' Dad spins around and checks for damage.

'It wasn't his fault. I started it.'

'Why, baby?'

I finally let myself cry. 'Because if I get what I deserve, then maybe Martin will come back.'

'Oh, Gracie. Haven't you learnt by now?' Mum asks. 'No one deserves to be hit. Whatever you've done, you don't ever deserve to be hit.'

***

All night I think about Martin's dad. I keep wondering what he'll say to his ex-wife if they speak. I can't think of a sentence long enough that will fill the time she left.

I don't want to leave all that space between me and the people I love. I can't talk to Martin, but at least I can try to fix things with Alyce. I can surrender my dignity and tell Jane that I need her, that her friendship is too important to throw away without even trying to save it.

'Mrs Iranian? Is Jane home?' I ask when I call on Wednesday morning.

'Gracie, it's good to hear from you. We were beginning to think you'd run away.' Some jokes just aren't funny, Mrs Iranian.

'No, I'm still here. Can I speak to Jane?'

'Hang on a minute, love. I'll get her for you.'

'Faltrain, what's up?' Her voice is clipped and short.

'I wanted to talk.'

'Let me guess. Something's wrong and you need help.'

'It is, Jane. Things are really, really bad.'

'Faltrain, why should I care what's wrong in your life when you couldn't care less what's happening in mine?'

'What? That's not fair.' I'm not the one who walked away. 'I care.'

'But you didn't care enough to call me back. I told you I needed to talk and you ignored me.'

'That's not why I didn't call. I thought you were busy with other stuff.'

'Other stuff?'

'You know, stuff other than me.'

'I was. I was busy with my life that exists away from you. If a tree falls in a forest and Gracie Faltrain doesn't hear it, you think it doesn't still fall?'

It's not like Jane to be cruel. 'Why are you so mad?'

'I'll say this slowly, so you'll understand. I have a life over here. In England. And it goes wrong just as much as yours does.'

'I doubt that . . .'

'Believe me, it does. And I've been trying to tell you about it for months, but you never listen.'

'Yes I do.'

'If I can find a gap in the conversation. Every time I try to tell you anything you cut me off and go on and on about Alyce and Martin and Flemming and Annabelle . . .'

'Are you jealous?' I ask.

'This is not about me being jealous.'

And then she's crying, and she's so far away. Jane never gets upset like this. She says stuff like, 'Suck it up, Faltrain,' when I get out of control. She's making up for lost time, today, hiccupping and snorting and choking, all together.

'When was the last time you asked me about me, Faltrain?'

I think. Believe me, I think hard. I want to be able to give her a time and date, to prove that after eleven years I'm as good at being a best friend as she is.

'I want to ask. I just forget, I guess. But that's not why I didn't call you again. I thought you didn't need me anymore . . .' My words drift on that ocean of silence sitting between us.

Of course, it's easy to see now. I'm an idiot. In a million

years Jane would never dump me. She's been there for me in every major event of my life. And the second she needed me, I bailed. That's crap. It's worse.

'What's crappier than crap, Jane?' I ask, hoping for a laugh to ease the tension.

'Gracie Faltrain?' she says.

'I guess I messed up. I'm sorry.' I've said that word a million times; half a million of them have been in the last few days. When you're really sorry, though, it's more than a word. It's a feeling in your chest heavy as rocks. You want to rip open your skin and empty them out.

'Why didn't you just tell me how dumb I was being, Jane? You have before. You know sometimes I'm an idiot.' Jane's always the one to pull me back when I've gone too far.

'I needed you to get it this time, Faltrain. I needed my best friend without having to ask for her.'

'I'm here now. Will you tell me what happened?'

I can feel her sigh from here. 'Life's so bad at the moment. I don't have anyone, and you've got Alyce and Martin and Flemming and Annabelle.'

'Annabelle?'

'Yeah, I even miss Annabelle Orion. That's how awful it is over here.'

'I thought things were okay. I thought you had heaps of friends.' So many you didn't need me.

'I did, at first. I fitted in because I was the new kid and I had this accent that everyone thought was funny. And then I guess I got a bit too popular, maybe, or one day I said the wrong thing . . . I don't know. But this year a girl called Veronica White started spreading rumours about me.'

'Like what?'

'Like I thought I was too good for everyone over here. Stuff like that, nothing big. But Faltrain, it only took a day for everyone to leave me. Twenty-four hours and I went from top of the charts to zero. It made me see that I don't have any real friends.'

'You have me.'

'It doesn't feel like it. I haven't had anyone to talk to in months. Do you know what that's like, Faltrain?'

No. I've always had her. Or Alyce. Or Martin.

'And you haven't even heard the worst of it. Veronica came up to me last month, and said she wanted to be friends again. She told me that Alexander Hood was dying to go out with me. And when I turned up for the date, half the kids in my class were there to watch me get stood up.'

'The oldest trick in the book,' I say.

'I know. It's in one in three teen movies.'

'I think it's closer to one in two.'

'And I fell for it. Hook, line, and sinking fast.' Jane sighs. 'I heard her say to the other kids that I deserved it. That I think I'm better than anyone else. I'm the butt of everyone's jokes, now. I spend every lunch in the library.'

'That sucks,' I say.

'You don't need to tell me that. I was mad at Veronica for a while, but then Mum said something that made a whole lot of sense. She told me that the Veronica Whites and the Annabelle Orions of the world are idiots. "They're the ones missing out, Janey. The world's three-dimensional. And they only see the surface. Anything deeper makes them scared."'

It hits me then that Jane and Alyce do have a whole lot in common after all, more than I do with either of them. Not because they're both hanging out in the library, but because they have the same way of looking at things.

People should be able to see the world from whatever angle they want. As long as they're not blocking anyone else's view. The stupid thing is, most of the time it's the loudest, roughest ones who get to see everything. People like Annabelle and Veronica and me, we elbow our way to the front, and get it all, the mountains, the oceans, the sky, the grass. And what do we do with it? We have a quick look and then turn around and laugh at the people who are standing at the back.

I guess that's why people like Alyce see the world differently. They have to make some stuff up. They spend a lot of time imagining what the view might be like. But you know, sometimes, when all you have of the sky before the sun drops is a quick glimpse of fire between the trees, it looks all that much brighter because of the black shapes in front of it.

I remember the day that Annabelle teased Jonathon Smith about his hair and Jane stood up for him. 'He should get a haircut,' I said. 'Or you're gonna have to spend your whole life as his bodyguard.'

'What right has she got to make him feel like crap, Faltrain? That kid can wear his hair any way he wants,' Jane had said. And she was right. She was smarter in Year 4 than I am in Year 11.

I've never really seen the big picture before. Never panned the camera up and seen how the world looks from long shot. Jane and Alyce and Susan, dumped before their big dates. Me and Annabelle and Veronica, tearing down anyone who isn't on our side.

'Are you still there, Faltrain? You've gone quiet.'

I take the deepest breath. Something tells me that after this question I might not come up for air for a long time.

'Is that me, Jane? Am I like Annabelle Orion?'

'You're not as close as I thought, if you're finally asking that question.'

I can't believe people on the other side of the world could see it and I'm just waking up now.

'Jane, what those people think, it doesn't mean anything.' For the first time all year, I actually believe that.

'I know. But thanks for saying it, Faltrain. You don't know how much I needed to hear it.'

'What would really fix you up is one of our all-night DVD sessions.'

'Get that player running, then.'

'I wish we could.'

'No, I mean it. I hadn't said anything yet because I was so angry at you. But Dad's flying back to Australia for a month. He said I could come with him.'

'You're coming home?'

'Don't get too excited. It's only for a month.'

I'm not proud. I'll take any bit of home I can get.

Jane listens now as I fill her in on everything that has happened. 'You are in way more trouble than me,' she says after I've finished.

'I thought I was helping.'

'I know. Deep down Martin and Alyce know that, too.'

'Do you think he'll come back?'

'I wouldn't give up hope yet. Martin Knight hasn't stopped looking at you since he saw you play soccer in Year 7. You just never noticed till last year. Wherever he is, you're with him, Faltrain. So are his dad and kid sister. I should know; you can move away, run away, it doesn't matter. Life sticks to you.'

'What if I never see him again?' I can cut back everything there is of me: the lies; treating Alyce like she's not good enough; hurting Jane. But I can't cut away what I did to Martin. I'll never come back if he doesn't. 'His dad and his sister will lose everything, Jane. Because of me.'

'Faltrain, this is bad, I won't lie and tell you anything different. You pushed him towards leaving. But he made the final decision. He didn't just all of a sudden think, "I can't cope with everything". He was coping a little less every day.'

'It's still my fault.' I'm quiet for a bit, but Jane hangs on, waiting for me to find the words to describe what's dragging me under the ocean like stones in my pockets. 'I can get to tomorrow,' I say. 'And the next day without him. But how do I get to next year and the year after that?'

'There's only one way to keep going, Faltrain. Fix what you can. And then find a way to live with the rest.'

'Jane,' I say before I hang up. 'I'm really, really sorry.' I may as well start fixing what I can, right now.

39

I've never felt more like cheering for her
than I do today. 'Go Gracie,' I shout.
Helen Faltrain

I'm on the freaking bench, Mum. Where is
it exactly that you want me to go?
Gracie Faltrain

Living with your mistakes isn't easy. Martin still isn't in goal today. Alyce's seat is still vacant. It makes the whole place feel empty.

I sit this game out on the bench like I have for the past three Saturdays. I don't want to be a part of the way they're playing anymore. If Martin comes back I want him to see that I've changed.

I hate the bench. It's hard and uncomfortable but it hurts my pride more than anything. Woodbury and his mates have a bye. They turn up to watch the game and make me feel like crap. 'This makes the third game that you've played from the bench, Faltrain. Too much for you, is it?' they say on the way past.

I want to tell them to get lost. I want to say that even if we lose this game we're still into the final, so shove that. I don't say anything, though. That sort of talk got us into this mess in the first place – even I can see that. And I'm looking to get out, not get in deeper.

Martin wanted me to walk away from the way I'd been playing and I wouldn't listen to him. I haven't listened to him all year. The only person I have been hearing is Gracie Faltrain. I can't take back the lies I've told. I can't take back looking for his mum. But I can do this for him. I figure after all I've done, it isn't too much to ask.

40

'If you're ever lost, Marty,' Mum always said when I was a kid and we were out together, 'go back to where we started. Go back and wait for me there.'
Martin Knight

For weeks I've sat in class wishing I was next to Alyce. Maybe I could be, but I don't have enough guts to ask. Every time she catches me staring she straightens her glasses and looks the other way.

I do more Alyce-watching than I've ever done in my life. All this time I've known her, I've only seen parts of the package. Her reading. Her weird taste in clothes. How bad she is at sport. But those things make her who she is. They make her funny. And smart. And strange. All the things I like about her.

She always opens the door for people. Everyone else barges through and Alyce waits until whoever is walking with her is safely on the other side. She's not letting herself get pushed around. She wants to do it.

She can walk from one side of the quadrangle to the other with her face in a book, and not bump into a thing.

She shares her lunch with Freddy Jabusi when he forgets his. They're eating together in the yard when I walk past this Friday. I want more than anything to stop and talk to her. To tell her how worried I am about Martin. She straightens her glasses. And I keep right on walking.

After school I walk to the same place I always do. To see Mr Knight.

'There's no news, Gracie,' he always says. I never stay long. Sometimes I go into Martin's room, act like I'm looking for clues to where he's gone. Really I just want to sit on his bed. Or do something stupid like smell his soccer shirt. I figure he must be coming back if he hasn't taken it. Martin wouldn't leave that behind.

It doesn't seem right that there isn't more being said about him. There were five minutes on the news the day after he left, and a couple of follow-up segments, but nothing else. I guess kids run away every day. At school we had the police come to ask us if we'd seen anything. Constable Blythe smiled at me. I kept my eyes down.

'Everyone knew him. Everyone liked him,' some kid said in that quick news segment. It's true. But it doesn't tell you enough. It doesn't describe how his hair always stuck up at the back or that when he said 'Faltrain' he opened his hands like he was trying to catch a wide ball in goal.

When I turn up at Martin's house tonight, Mr Knight pulls out a chair for me to sit down on. 'There's news?' I ask.

The last thing Mr Knight told me was that the police had found Martin's mum, Alison. Mr Knight said her name like a language he knew once, but hadn't spoken in years. 'She hasn't seen him, Gracie,' he said. And disappointment coated his face. Tonight he has a look of hope, though.

'There was a sighting of a boy fitting Martin's description buying a ticket to Dromana.'

'Where's that?'

'It's a little town near the beach. It's the last place we went on holidays together before Alison left. Did Martin ever tell you about it?'

I wish I could say yes, for both our sakes. 'Sorry, Mr Knight.'

'I remember us being happy there, those two weeks. It was like everything that was bothering Alison stayed in the city. When we drove away, the only thing in the car was the four of us.

'Martin and his mum spent most of the time in the rock pools. I took the kids to the surf beach a few times, dunked them in and pulled them out. Marty said it felt like a washing machine. His mum said, "How would you know what it feels like inside there?" Every day was fine. Every day was warm. Alison said the sky was the colour of bird eggs; I've never forgotten that. The rain didn't start until the last day, when we were leaving.

'I'm going to find him, Gracie.' After he says that, I notice two old suitcases sitting near the table. 'I should have gone to find him a long time ago.'

'Martin told me that you were trying. He was happy about that, Mr Knight. I'm the one who didn't think it was good enough.' If it were me, I'd want my dad to know that I hadn't doubted him.

'He's a good kid. But I only met him halfway after the Championships.' A car horn sounds from out the front. He looks at his watch. 'Karen!' he calls. 'That's our taxi. We have a train to catch. This time,' he says, brushing my shoulder with his hand, 'I'm going the whole way. Karen and me and Martin, we're coming back together.'

Karen walks into the kitchen and picks up her suitcase. It looks too heavy in her hand. Mr Knight reaches out and carries it for her.

If Dad's right and cyclones start over warm oceans, then the last place the Knights were happy together is where Martin's storm started. A part of it, anyway. Some of the bad weather came from me; I know that now.

If Mr Knight has a chance to undo all of the damage that's been done, it makes sense to go back to where the rain and wind began. He can't stop the cyclone now that it has started. But he can look at the patterns. Maybe he can stop it from happening again.

41

I am a *dog.*
Alyce Fuller

If Mr Knight has the guts to go to Dromana, I can pick up the phone.

'Hi, Mrs Fuller. Is Alyce there?'

'Gracie, love, she just left. She's gone to the dance.'

'With Flemming? I mean Andrew?'

'No, dear. She went on her own. Her dad drove her. She looked so beautiful.'

'I bet she did, Mrs Fuller.'

I don't waste time getting changed.

Alyce is stepping out of the car when Mum and I drive up. She's wearing this dress that cuts in at the waist and flares out, dark blue with silver around the edges. It's the colour of night-time, full of stuff too far away to see: acres of stars, and black holes and burning galaxies. She looks amazing, a hundred times better than when she was wearing that dress I picked out for her in the shop. A million times better than anyone else here.

Flemming thinks so, too. He might be holding Susan's hand, but it's Alyce he can't stop staring at. He's got the same look in his eye that he has on the soccer field when he knows he's kicked wrong and lost his chance for goal.

I edge my way towards her. Try to look casual. 'Hi, Alyce. Great dress,' I say.

'Nice jeans,' she answers. Her voice doesn't belong to the Alyce I know, or maybe it does. One thing I've worked out: I haven't been listening very hard to the world. I've been listening to my commentary on it, and it hasn't quite matched the game.

'Alyce, I wanted to say sorry, about everything.'

'Sorry that Martin's gone and it's your fault? Sorry that for the past year you've been trying to make me into Jane, so you don't feel embarrassed hanging out with me? Or sorry that you've been caught and we don't want anything to do with you anymore?'

'I don't care that you're a nerd, Alyce.' That sounded much better in my head. 'What I meant to say was that you don't need to change to be my friend.' Again, not exactly how I imagined that sounding.

'You are unbelievable, Gracie Faltrain. You think you're so much better than anyone else.'

'I don't. Not anymore.' This isn't going how I planned. I blame the flashing disco lights. I blame the boogie.

'I guess to someone like you, I must look pretty ordinary,' she says.

I take a minute to let her words sink in. They should. A person who treats their friends like I have should feel it in their blood.

'I make you feel bad?'

'Most of the time. It's pretty hard living up to how you want the world to be.'

'I'm the one who's going to change.'

'I don't want you to change, Gracie. I want you to stop trying to change everyone else.'

'I will.' I know that tonight is just the start, though. Those two words are like a kid's song. They don't mean a whole lot without some actions to go along with them.

Her eyes drift across to Flemming. 'Look, he's holding Susan's hand.' Alyce's heart was clean and shiny before Flemming and now there's about 200,000 kilometres on the speedo. It needs some oil and water. Let's face it, after what I did, she probably needs a new starter motor.

'I'm sorry, Alyce. You wouldn't feel so bad now if it wasn't for me.'

'I just wish I hadn't hoped so hard that he'd like me. When he asked me to the dance, he said, "I reckon you're the smartest person I know, Fuller". Then he kissed me. I could smell grass and popcorn. I thought I could smell the sky on a windy day. I had all these kites in my chest, moving around, trying to get out. I bet that sounds stupid to you,' she says. 'I bet you think I'm stupid because no one's ever wanted to kiss me before.'

'No, Alyce. I don't think that.'

'And then he took it all back. He came up to me in the classroom and I thought he was going to kiss me again. And then he said I was boring. That all I did was read. And I told him that it was okay.'

'Alyce, he did like you, he just didn't have the guts to admit it.'

'But then it doesn't mean anything, does it? If he didn't like me enough not to care what everyone else thinks of me. Why do they all treat me like that?' she asks.

If she'd asked me that question a month ago, even two

weeks ago, I would have said, 'They treat you like that, Alyce, because you let them.' But that's not the real reason at all.

'You're different, Alyce. And they don't know what to do with you. You're better than them.'

'Love sucks, doesn't it?' she asks after a while.

'You've been hanging out with me way too long. Do you want to dance?'

Alyce has a great way of moving. She throws her arms out like she's spraying confetti. I never even knew she could dance. My style involves more kicking and punching. Faster than Alyce. Different, but not better. She spins out and lets the skirt of her dress twirl wide. I can feel it for a second, brushing against my jeans.

Corelli comes over to us and starts to dance next to Alyce. 'Hey, Corelli,' Singh calls out. 'You move like a washing machine.'

Corelli goes red. 'Shut up, loser.'

Alyce saves him, though. She starts moving her arms around in a spin cycle. The four of us laugh and spin and kick and punch in turns.

Flemming has dropped Susan's hand. He's moving back and forth, like he's almost decided to walk over to Alyce, but then can't quite get up the guts to do it. You idiot, I think, you're missing all of this. But I'm not too hard on him. Let's face it; he's not alone in the stuffing up department.

'Dog,' Newman shouts to Alyce on his way past.

She stops dancing and for a second I think the night is ruined. Forget him, Alyce, I'm about to say, when Corelli calls out over the music, 'You are a *dog*.' He says it like it's the best thing in the world to be, and then spins around like the big idiot he is. But Alyce loves it. She's happy. This would all be perfect, if Martin was okay.

'I have to go, Alyce,' I say. I can feel the song and the lights echoing round my chest.

'I'll come with you,' she answers. Mum was right. Alyce's friendship is worth fighting for. I'm glad that I did.

Flemming is standing with Annabelle as we leave. 'I have to go to the bathroom. Meet you out the front,' Alyce says as we walk past them.

'Hey,' he calls to me. 'Still no word about Knight?'

'His dad thinks he might have gone to Dromana. They went there on holidays when he was a kid.'

'I'd run away too, if Gracie Faltrain was my girlfriend,' Annabelle says.

'Shut up,' Flemming yells at her, and takes a step towards me. 'He'll be okay, Faltrain.'

But I deserved what Annabelle said. If everything was the other way around, and she'd done what I had, I'd say something like that too. I'd say worse. I swallow any pride that I have left. 'Did he ever tell you about the holiday?' I ask her.

Maybe she sees how sad I am. Maybe for the first time in my life I'm not threatening to punch her. She looks at me and shakes her head. She seems, sort of, real.

'I saw Susan in the toilets,' Alyce says while we're waiting outside the hall for Dad to pick us up.

'Did she say anything to you?'

'No. She seemed sad. So I told her that her dress looked pretty.'

You know how people tell you that one tiny bit of sweet, dark chocolate is better than a truck full of the cheap stuff? Well, Alyce is Lindt. That's why Flemming had to ask her to the dance. That's why he'll feel sick later. Because he's had about a block and a half of Susan tonight, when he could have had the tiniest piece of the real thing.

***

Dad waits for Alyce to walk inside and then starts the car again.

'Did Mr Knight call while I was out?'

'Sorry, baby. Give him a bit of time – he'll have barely arrived.' He taps his fingers against the steering wheel. 'Gracie, I wanted to tell you how proud I am.'

'Of me?'

'It's not easy living with your mistakes. I should know. And it's not easy to lose the things you love.'

'Mum doesn't think I'm doing so great.'

'Don't be so sure. After she dropped you off tonight she was crying.'

'How come?'

'My guess is that she missed you. And now she knows you're on the way back.'

42

The world looks a whole lot different
standing in someone else's soccer boots.
Gracie Faltrain

No one wants to admit that Martin still won't be here today. This is the decider. If we win this, then we're into the final.

'Faltrain,' Coach says. 'I know you miss Knight. I know that playing without him is hard. But I need you out there.'

I nod. 'I'll take his spot, then. In goal.' He doesn't argue. He just shifts Maiden into the midfield.

I figure I owe it to Martin to see what his life has been like, what he's been trying to tell me all this time. If he ever comes back I want to prove to him that I'm listening.

All this time I thought Martin was a coward. But the game he's been playing is harder than I thought. I'm on the lookout for attack all through the first half. If I let my guard down for a second then they'll score. Do that too many times and the game's over. Almost all of Martin's life has been defence. Looking after his family, and me. Guarding the last memories of his mum. I wanted him to attack so badly, kick his dad to wake him up. Kick the other team in soccer.

But standing in Martin's place today, I see that attack can be ugly. Flemming smacks into players and flips them like pancakes, flat on their backs. Sure, he gets the ball and scores three goals in a row. But he used to do that all the time. He just never hurt other players to do it.

The thing is, I've watched these guys play since Year 7. I know their style. Flemming could have made at least two of those goals by cutting to the right at the centre of the field and then swinging into the gap left by one of their defenders. Sure, the degree of difficulty was high, but man, what a great goal it would have been if he'd made it.

I guess up until now, I haven't been able to work out what I think. Those guys did set the rules. But we set some before them. Like I said, human nature's like a track on loop. But someone's got to stop it.

'Francavilla,' I say at half time, 'you're playing like you don't want to be out there, I can tell.'

'I don't want to be. It's no fun anymore. I used to love protecting goal, predicting the shots, making sure no one got through. It's not the same anymore. I'm thinking I might sign up for footy next year.'

'Fair enough.' I don't even try to convince him to stay. I know exactly what he means.

We went from man to ape in one season. 'Blows the theory of evolution right out of the water, doesn't it, Faltrain?' It feels good to have Jane's voice back in my head. It hasn't just been man to ape, either. It's been woman to ape woman. Whatever. I've been in there kicking as much as the next guy.

Sometimes you have to stand back a bit to get the full picture. And the one I'm seeing today in the second half? It's full of bad soccer players. We're nothing like we were.

Except for a guy called Jason Harroway. He's scoring goals for the opposition like he's playing for Brazil. I know him because in Year 8 he came to some of our practices. He hadn't made it onto a team at his school and his dad knew Coach. 'Nice shot,' he'd say to me as I sank a goal. He never hassled me about being a girl. Everyone on our team liked him.

Seeing him play this afternoon makes me want to rewind, cut back to when I sank goals without sinking the other players. I want to be the best because I'm good. Not because our team's a pack of thugs.

Jason takes the ball from Corelli, and it makes him enemy number one, no matter what he's done in the past. He steals it fair and square. No rough stuff. It's a beautiful thing to see. Real soccer. His foot edges in quiet, like a thief. Once he has it he runs, moving like he's on blades, gliding to goal.

Flemming races at him with the momentum of a rock rolling down a huge hill. Harroway doesn't see him coming. 'Jason,' I call out from goal, but it's too late. Flemming slams at him in the middle of the field. From here it looks like a block tackle, but I know better. Jason is the other team's chance at winning. So Flemming takes him out.

As they both fall down, Flemming's knee connects with Jason's nose. The ball spins out. The other team gets an indirect free kick. Harroway gets an ambulance. Flemming pretty much gets away with it.

He shouldn't have. The game keeps going and in the background, I can see the ambulance guys close the doors and drive away. And I'm not the only one who's looking. The rest of our team shuffles around, like they've been sleepwalking, and all of a sudden they've woken up somewhere strange. The thing is, when you're heavy with night, it's hard to get back to where you should be.

After the game finishes, Coach rubs his eyes like he's tired of seeing. He doesn't even say congratulations, you won. You're into the final. 'I'm going to the hospital,' he says more to Flemming than the rest of us. 'I'll call you when I know something.'

'Call him at my place,' I tell him. 'He's coming home with me.'

'The ref ruled it as an accident,' Flemming says as we wait in my kitchen for the news. He locks his hands together and bangs them softly on the table.

'It wasn't, Flemming. I saw it. I saw you threatening that guy at the back of the change rooms, too.'

'He hit Corelli. I was protecting the team, making sure no one else got their heads ripped off. The guy was an idiot.'

'Don't give me that. You were enjoying yourself.'

'So what if I was? We're gonna win the finals, Faltrain. And every scout in the place will be there. You and me both know the only thing we've got going for us is soccer.'

'They won't pick us if we're playing like thugs.'

'So make sure you don't get caught on TV kicking some guy in the balls.'

'Listen to yourself. The whole reason you play soccer is that you love the game. And now you're saying it's all right to play dirty as long as no one sees, as long as we win?'

Flemming keeps tapping his fist on the table.

'What if Jason's hurt, really hurt? You knew him this time, Flemming. He wasn't an idiot. He was a mate.'

'I want to win so bad, Faltrain. I want to play for the state.

You were right about the school stuff, about me being stupid. I'm not gonna pass Year 12. I'm barely passing Year 11. I've got nothing else.'

'You're not stupid, Flemming.'

'I know what I am. Even my dad says I'm not going anywhere.'

If there are buttons you can push to ruin someone, there are ones you can push to fix them. They're harder to find, though. Flemming's not an idiot. He's just done some stupid things. There's a difference.

'We'll win, Flemming. I promise. We'll thrash them on our terms. In front of everyone, we'll prove we can do it. Imagine all the talent scouts seeing that.'

As soon as I say it I feel that old excitement building up in me again. I imagine soaring along the grass, heading to Flemming, kicking to Singh, scoring goals like a champion.

'You're dreaming, Faltrain,' he says.

'Maybe. But they won't pick you for state playing like you are, and you know it. Any scout there today would've scratched you off the list. But the old you, the Flemming who plays soccer better than anyone I've seen, they'd take in a second.'

'Better than anyone?'

'Except me, of course.'

The phone rings before he can answer. Mum walks in to pick it up. Dad walks in behind her and sits with us at the table.

Flemming's whole body freezes, caught in ice. I know that feeling. He's about to find out if he's hurt someone else too bad to fix. It's a cold feeling. It's lonely.

'Yes. Yes,' Mum says. Her face is hard to read. Dad reaches out across the table and holds my hand. 'I'll let them know. Thanks, Coach.'

She hangs up and turns to us. 'He's awake. A broken nose, concussion,' she lists his injuries off on her fingers, 'and a dislocated finger. He's going to be okay, Andrew. The doctor said he's going to be fine.'

'All right,' Flemming says, and I can hear in his voice a change of direction.

'Harroway's a better player than he was in Year 8, Faltrain.' Flemming and I are waiting on the steps for his dad to come. 'Did you see the way he took the ball off Corelli?'

'Like taking candy from a baby,' I say. 'I miss playing like that.'

Flemming stands up as his dad arrives. 'I miss it too, Faltrain.'

'So we're playing like we used to in the final?' I ask.

'Just remember. You promised we'd win.'

We will. And it will be even better than last season. Because winning means a whole lot more when you know what it feels like to lose.

In my dream tonight, Martin is sleeping in the middle of the road. There are cars racing past. He's about to be hit, but I can't scream loud enough to wake him. There's something caught in my throat and I can't make a sound. All I can do is watch and hope that he wakes up in time. At the end of the dream, a car drives right over the top of him. Martin doesn't die. He disappears. That's when the thing in my throat vanishes. Every vocal chord comes alive and I'm screaming for all I'm worth. But it's too late.

Mum shakes me. 'You're dreaming, wake up.'

I blink into the half light of my bedroom. 'What time is it?'

'Six o'clock. Mr Knight is on the phone.'

His voice is low, crouching with sleep. 'I've found him, love,' he says. 'I'm bringing him home.'

He hangs up, but before he does I imagine I can hear the sound of the ocean. And it's calm.

43

Alyce Fuller: one. Gracie Faltrain: zero.
Alyce Fuller

The world is a good place today. I can feel spring hanging at the edges. 'He's on his way home, Alyce,' I say at the start of sport.

'That's fantastic news, Gracie.' And then she does something that's never been done before. Alyce Fuller plays with the laws of the universe. She raises her hand and volunteers to be captain. She smiles at the look on my face. 'You're not the only one who gets to set the rules,' she says.

'So how come you never did that before?'

'Because I never wanted to be a captain. But today, I feel like it.'

Good for you, Alyce. I'm not happy because she's starting to act like everyone else. I don't care about that. I'm happy because she's smiling. I put my hand up as well.

'Freddy Jabusi,' she calls when it's her turn. She picks every crap player in the class. Corelli's the only guy on her team who's even close to okay. She chooses her final player and smiles as he walks over. She makes him feel like the first. It's in how you choose, I guess, not in the choosing.

I have Flemming and Maiden and Singh. I have Susan and Annabelle. I call her name last, but I follow Alyce's lead. I try as hard as I can to give her a grin on the way past. My smile moves like a rusty bike. She stares at me as if I'm crazy. Being nicer to Annabelle could take a little practice.

It should be an easy game of basketball. We're clearly the better players, no offence to Alyce's team. We lose, though. Maybe it's because Flemming keeps passing her the ball. I don't bother reminding him that he's on my side.

'Congratulations, Alyce,' I say at the end, shaking her hand.

'And congratulations to you, Gracie.'

'What for? We didn't win.'

'You've been chosen for the comedy debate. You and I are speaking in it this afternoon.'

'What?' The day gets about a hundred degrees colder.

'Gracie Faltrain isn't scared of talking at assembly, is she? They'll love you.'

Alyce Fuller: one. Gracie Faltrain: zero.

There's something about public speaking that bothers me. I think it's the fear of wetting my pants in front of an audience of about a million people.

'Alyce,' I whisper. 'I have to pee again.'

Gracie, some of those kids out there can probably lip-read, she writes on the paper in front of her. Good point. I smile as wide as I can.

Don't worry, I have a plan, she writes.

I keep smiling. There's an auditorium full of kids waiting for me to speak. A good time to let me in on the plan would be, say, NOW, Alyce. It crosses my mind that her plan might be to teach me a lesson. I don't need to learn any more. I've learnt enough. But I guess that I was happy for Alyce to experience this humiliation so that she could grow as a person, so in the words of Jane, 'Suck it up, Faltrain. You deserve this.'

I look down at the topic again. 'School teaches us nothing. The real world is where we learn the most.'

The hardest part is that this crowd expects to be entertained. It's not like other debates. There's only one rule: you have to be funny or you never live it down. That's why kids like Annabelle do it. Every-one is too scared not to laugh. She'd kill them afterwards. But Alyce and me? We really have to be funny. Either that or we're dead. I have to admit, this was not one of my better ideas.

I don't have a speech, I write to Alyce. My letters are shaky. I'm getting hysterical now. I'm the middle speaker.

I told you before, you don't need one, she writes back just before her name is called.

'The first speaker for the affirmative. Alyce Fuller.'

'Good afternoon everyone,' Alyce says. Her voice is shaky. She's tapping her left foot, like she always does when she's nervous. I concentrate on sending her every last good vibe that's in me.

'I'm here to prove to you today that school teaches us nothing. My team and I are differing from the standard rules of the debate where I speak first, and then the next person speaks and then the third. We would stick to those rules, but we have no idea how a real debate works. Andrew Flemming was talking too loudly during that lesson for us to hear what Mrs Wilson was saying, so we actually don't know how to debate.'

Alyce clicks the computer and a huge picture of Flemming fills the screen above us. He's leaning back on his chair and reaching out to hit Corelli. Everyone laughs. I can see Flemming cracking up in the back row. He loves being the centre of attention. Alyce laughs right along with everyone. Her hands have stopped shaking. Her foot is still.

'To demonstrate how little we actually learn in school today, I'm going to use my second speaker. What is your name?' Alyce turns to me.

'Huh?' I say, not catching on to my role in all of this.

Alyce shakes her head. 'See, absolutely nothing has sunk in. Your name?'

'Oh. Gracie Faltrain.'

'Good.' People are laughing, but I don't care. They think it's scripted. Alyce winks at me. 'Name the last five prime ministers of Australia.'

I play up my part. Shake my head. Look dumb. It's not all an act, I have to tell you. I have no idea who the last five prime ministers were.

'Name the elements in the periodic table.'

'Yeah, right. Like that's ever going to happen.' I start enjoying the laughter rushing up like a wave.

'But if I asked you to name the country that won the World Cup in 2002 . . .'

'Brazil defeated Germany two–nil.' I spin the fact off without thinking.

Alyce nods and turns to face the audience. 'Proof that it is not school that teaches us, but the real world.' She waits for quiet and then turns around to Fran Walker, our third speaker.

'Name five American poets.'

Fran looks blank.

'Four Australian ones?'

Blanker.

'Two explorers that climbed Mount Everest? One of the first countries to give women the right to vote?'

Blankest. Fran plays her part beautifully. She is a crisp, white, clean piece of paper that has never been written on.

Annabelle is up next. And even I can see; she has nowhere to go. People are on Alyce's side. Finally, they can see how funny and smart she is.

Annabelle walks to the centre of the stage after she has been introduced. She smiles that smile that tells me she has something up her sleeve. 'Firstly, I'd like to rebut some of the opposition's arguments.' She turns to Alyce. 'Name four American poets.'

Oh no. Unless Alyce lies, she'll have to answer that question. She must be the only kid in our school who has answers like that swimming around in her brain. See where education gets you? It loses a person the debate. It's dangerous.

I look across to Alyce and wait for her next move. She smiles back at Annabelle and then faces the audience. 'I'll name five. Auden, Aiken, Ashbery, Bly and Cummings . . . But let's face it. I'm the biggest nerd in the school. I want everyone out there in the audience to ask yourselves the question: would you know the answer?'

And everyone laughs. Not for Annabelle. For Alyce. I catch sight of Flemming. He's standing up and clapping. I point him out to her. 'Are you going to give him a second chance?' I whisper.

'I don't think so, Gracie,' she says. And as everyone's clapping, she stands up and takes a bow.

The scores are even, Alyce, I think, as a thousand people clap for her. I couldn't have asked for a clearer sign. Except I shouldn't have needed one. Martin was right. I have treated

Alyce like dirt. I wanted her to be like all the rest of the kids in the school. But then she wouldn't be as great as she is. What sort of person needs the whole school to applaud her best friend to prove that she's great? I remember last year, when no one was clapping for me, Martin and Alyce were still there, cheering me on. Because I was Gracie Faltrain. And that was enough for them.

And who's applauding for you now? I think. Alyce turns to me and Fran and waves at us to stand up, too. Fran does, but I shake my head. Some days you don't deserve applause. But Alyce grabs my arm and drags me up. 'Smile, Gracie. We won,' she says. No Alyce. You did.

44

Game over.
Martin Knight

Everyone files out of the hall. Usually most of the kids leave for home pretty quickly, but today after the debate there's a small crowd still hanging around near the front of the school.

'Some of your fans, Alyce,' I tease her.

She looks at the kids. 'Gracie,' she says softly, and that smile of hers finally takes off. 'Look.'

The crowd clears a little, and I see Martin, laughing with Francavilla and Singh and Corelli. Flemming is hanging around, too. Martin's wearing the t-shirt I gave him for Christmas. His hands are hooked into the edges of his pockets like always. He still hasn't brushed his hair. On the outside he's exactly the same. Except now I can't go up to him. Now there's a fence between us.

'Go on,' I say to Alyce. 'Go and say hi.'

'You don't want to come?'

More than I've wanted anything in my entire life. 'I'll see you tomorrow,' I say. Every step I take hurts. Because no one follows me.

The sky is messy this afternoon, cut with colours bleeding into each other. When I was a kid I remember making paintings that looked like that. Everyone else was using a brush, but I wanted to dig my hands in and smear the colour on the page. That's how I feel inside these days, because everyone's telling me that I'm the one who stuffed up.

And I did. I lied. I tried to change Alyce. I fought on that field like Flemming, and I saw how ugly that was. And there was a part of me that liked it. Loved it.

There's a part of me that's glad Martin and his dad are talking, whatever the cost. But I know that you can't take people's lives and make them how you want them to be, because if you do that, then it's not their life anymore. And what's the point of living if someone else is calling all the plays? But it's hard to sit on the bench and see that the people you love are hurting. Especially when you think you could fix things, push a few people aside so they can look at the view.

Alyce and Martin kept piling on those layers to block out the sun because it hurt them, I guess. And they kept telling me that it did, but I kept pushing them out there even though they were burning. Mum said that night we watched the mice on the Discovery Channel that she couldn't bear to see them experimented on.

'It's for the good of science,' I said.

'A lot of things get done for the greater good, Gracie. It doesn't make them right.'

I don't hear Martin this afternoon until he's close behind me. 'I always know where to find you, Faltrain.' He lies down next to me, one elbow bent beneath him so he can look out at the field.

'So I heard you guys are through to the final.'

'It's on Saturday. Are you playing?'

'I don't know, Faltrain. I haven't decided.'

I wait for a bit, but he doesn't say anything else. 'You're still mad at me, aren't you?'

'Yeah. But not as mad as when I left.' His eyes catch cars on the street and watch them till they disappear.

'Your dad said you went to the beach.' Every word I say is a footstep in the dark.

Martin's voice stays steady, though. 'It was an accident, sort of. I got to the station and saw Dromana on the destination board and bought a ticket. I guess Dad told you we had our last holiday there.'

'He said your mum seemed happy.'

'She did. We spent most days crouched over the rock pools. "It's a whole other world in there, Marty", I remember her saying. "Full of things that are too tiny to see."

'She loved me and Karen,' he says, biting down on the words in case they escape. 'Some things you have to feel, I reckon, and I felt it on that holiday. She spent every second she had with us. Reading us stories, walking along the beach, talking. One night she fell asleep on the bed with me, still holding my hand. I remember waking up, and seeing her there. I'd forgotten most of that, until I went back. I guess that holiday was her way of saying goodbye.'

'Did you talk to your dad about it?'

Martin nods. 'He and Karen found me lying on the beach. I haven't seen them smile like that since before Mum left. After Karen went to bed, Dad sat up with me in the hotel. He told me stuff that hurt him to say. "She was happy, on that holiday, Marty", he told me. "But I knew it was the last time we'd have her like that."' Martin fights off tears as he talks.

'"I knew her inside out", Dad said. "And the saddest thing is she couldn't have won. She'd have died if she'd stayed. And leaving would have killed her. Wherever she is, Marty, she's broken. I can't bear to think of her like that." He cried, Faltrain. Do you know what it's like to see your old man look like a kid?'

'Martin . . .'

'Don't tell me you're sorry. I don't want to hear that again.' He pulls his knees up to his chin, and keeps chasing those cars with his eyes. If he could, he'd be in one of them. Not here.

'I noticed you way before you noticed me,' he says after a while. 'I was following you around the whole time you were chasing that idiot Nick Johnson. I loved watching you play soccer. I loved watching you.'

'We're playing that way again, Martin, like we did at the start. Flemming and me and the rest of the team, we decided you were right. I shouldn't have done what I did; I shouldn't have found your mum when it was none of my business.'

'I know you didn't make all of this mess, Faltrain.' His hands are trying to catch that wide ball again. They look like he's trying to build something out of the air, a reason for the way I acted. 'But you lied to me. All year. I told you stuff I never told anyone else. I trusted you. Why was it so important to you that I find her?'

'I thought you'd stopped caring about soccer. I thought you'd given up.'

'And that wasn't good enough for you, Faltrain, was it? You couldn't have a boyfriend in goal. What if I said you were right? I have given up on soccer. What if after I read that note from Mum all the stuff she used to tell me about life just seemed like lies, and I couldn't play anymore, because it hurt too much imagining her at the games? Am I good enough for you now?'

'Yes, Martin.'

'But that's the crap thing. It's too late now. I know I said I couldn't understand how you leave the people you love. But sometimes you have to. Sometimes it's the only way to keep going.'

I know now what Martin's mum meant when she said people are all desperate for something. They're desperate to win, so mad for it they'd drag people back, just so it looks like they're going forwards. But not everyone can win.

The light fades. Neither of us moves. When one of your best friends is leaving, it's worth stretching it out as long as you can.

In the movies there's always that bit where the person gets dumped and you see how bad they feel. In books too. They describe how their heart aches. How they feel like they never want to get out of bed again. How the sun doesn't shine anymore.

Well, anyone who's ever been dumped can tell you that those descriptions are a whole lot of crap. They don't come anywhere close to telling it how it really is. One minute you're on the soccer field, flying for goal. And then the next minute the ground is empty. It's dark. And you've got no one to kick to but yourself.

'How was practice tonight, baby?' Dad asks when I get home.

'I wasn't at practice. I was with Martin.'

'So, did you find out the end of his story now that he's back?'

'Yeah, I know how it ends. He dumps me.'

'That's not the real ending, though, is it, Gracie?'

'No. He gets closer to his dad, and works out stuff about his mum.'

'So the ending is happy for Martin.'

'But it's not happy for me.'

'You're not the hero of his story, Gracie. It doesn't have to be happy for you.'

Dad looks out the window of my room. 'Your mother planted this part of the garden especially for you. She wanted it to grow in crowded tangles all around the window. "I want her to have a life full of everything, Bill", she said.'

'Did she want it full of sad stuff, too?'

'A little sad stuff is okay. As long as it doesn't choke everything else. You'll get over Martin, even though it doesn't feel like it.'

'What if I don't want to get over him? What if I want him back?'

'Do you think you deserve him?'

Good shot, Dad. You've been taking lessons from Mum. 'No,' I say.

'Then maybe you have a chance. Baby, I know better than anyone, you can always turn the ship around. Look at me. Slowly change direction, Gracie. Maybe one day Martin will trust you again.'

Dad's right. If I want Martin back, it's going to take time. Lots of it.

'Look,' Dad says, pointing through a gap to the middle of the garden. 'I think the magnolia's about to come out.'

'Dinner's been on the table for ten minutes, you two,' Mum yells from the kitchen. 'Now move it and set the table.'

You're absolutely right, Dad. I'd say that for you, the magnolia is well on the way.

And for me? Maybe I have to wait a while longer. I pruned a little late this year. The great thing about spring is it loops like everything else. Martin will still be around next season, and the one after. I've got all that time to prove to him that I've changed.

But that doesn't mean I'm not going to start straightaway.

45

It's not over till it's over.
Gracie Faltrain

'So we're all still sure this is the way we want to play it?' Flemming asks before the final.

'I'm sure,' I say, and everyone else nods. There's no other way we can go out there and win.

'It means we have to be better than ever before. It's Woodbury we're up against. He still wants us dead.' Flemming looks at us all to make sure we're hearing him properly. 'The scouts are out there. The match is being televised. It could be humiliating.'

'It's been a humiliating season,' Singh says. 'It's time to turn it around.'

'Then I guess I'll see you all in hospital after the game,' Flemming says. He turns to Coach, who's smiling next to him. 'So tell us again how you think we should play it?'

The stands are full. Alyce and Mum and Dad are right in the front. 'I've got 000 plugged into my phone,' Mum said earlier.

'Thanks,' I told her. 'That makes me feel a whole lot better.'

There's still no sign of Martin.

'Did you call him, Flemming?'

'For the fiftieth time, Faltrain. I called. He said he'd make it.'

I guess it doesn't matter. I'd do this even if he wasn't here to watch.

'Stop staring, Corelli. I told you before: they're not real.'

'I'm not staring at them. I've just never seen you nervous before.'

I'm gutsy. I'm not an idiot. Woodbury and his thugs are warming up on the field and they look ready. Our team looks ready to run more than anything else. But sooner or later you have to change the play. If you don't, everyone keeps saying the same lines over and over again.

'You sure about this?' Flemming asks. 'You stand to lose more body parts than any of us. You're smaller and you're a target.'

'I'm sure.' A woman with a camera takes a picture of us from the side of the field. Her camera whirrs and clicks. What's worse than total humiliation? Total humiliation on the front page of the paper. Total humiliation on TV.

'Ready to die, Faltrain?' Woodbury asks me on his way past.

'Look, I know you're angry about the off-season games. I get that. But what about calling it even, today?'

'Get lost,' he says, and I can't blame him. I had to try, though. It always works in the movies.

'You need to be ready for a fight. A fair fight,' Coach said in his pep talk. 'Create space the way we used to. Listen to each other the way you used to. Play like you're playing for the state. And there's a chance you just might.'

Fat chance of that, Coach, I think as the whistle blows. Let the games begin.

Flemming kicks off. We all run. I get to the ball first. I don't have time to take it, though. 'Faltrain, to your left,' Singh yells. Woodbury slams me in the shoulder and keeps running. The ball is glued to his foot until he scores. I'm still on the ground when he drives it home.

I'm aching already, but I drag myself up. Maiden mouths 'Sorry' at me from the goal. 'Don't worry,' I yell. It's not his fault. We knew this was going to be tough.

We start again. I'm a kid in the ocean, waves thumping over me, salt pumping into my mouth. I can't keep my face above water. I can taste blood from my fall.

I only get the ball once in the first half. I'm moving fast, but I'm surrounded. Someone shoves me in the back and I go down. I don't see who does it, but as I'm lying there a foot sinks into my stomach. I curl up on the ground as the whistle goes.

'What the hell are you playing at out there?' Martin yells in the break when I limp to the edge of the field.

'You've been watching?' I ask.

'Yeah, I've been watching. You're lucky to be alive.'

'We're playing like you told us, Martin.'

'You idiot, Faltrain.'

'What?' I'm nursing a hernia here for you, Knight. 'Don't call me an idiot.'

Martin's voice is like a magnet, drawing the rest of the team in. 'I didn't tell you to lie down out there and let them run right over the top of you. They're ahead by three goals. I said don't fight dirty. I didn't say don't fight.'

'What are you saying we should do?' Flemming asks. He's ready to follow again. And Martin is all geared up to lead. I love it. I feel like yelling across to that photographer, 'Make sure you get a picture of this.'

Martin keeps talking as he pulls on his soccer top. 'Faltrain, you want to sit this one out?'

'No way.'

'Good. We need you in there. Wrecker, you swap with me for a while. You look like you could do with a rest. Now everyone, listen in. You have to play like we used to. We knew exactly what everyone else on the team was thinking last year. I could predict, down to the last second, when Faltrain was about to run for goal. She'd flick her leg back to give herself a bit of momentum and go. Corelli, how do you know when Singh is about to kick the ball to you?'

'He runs at me and says, "Corelli".'

'Don't be smart. What else?'

'He looks like he's about to fart.'

'I'm concentrating,' Singh whines.

'Yeah. And it looks like you're about to fart.'

'We need to go back to how we used to be, moving like parts of the same car. Forget that they're willing to take you out. Start playing how we did in the Championships and they won't have time to knock us down. They won't have time for anything at all.'

'I've got your back, Faltrain,' Martin says while we're waiting for the ref to start us.

'Same goes for me,' I answer. 'I thought you'd given up on soccer.'

'I've changed my mind. For today.'

It's a small sign, but I'll take it.

Their midfielder takes the ball after kick-off, but Flemming slides across and steals it. And then he sends it to me. I move fast, confident. Woodbury runs at me again. He thinks he knows me. He thinks I'll send the ball to the right. I flick it to the inside of my left foot, instead. At the last minute I move it to the outside. By the time Woodbury realises I'm passing the other way, it's too late. Martin has it. And he's heading towards goal.

He gets there and he's surrounded. But we all know what to do. Coach taught us years ago. We fan out and the opposition follows. Martin kicks to me. I kick back to him. He's facing the wrong way, but I know what he'll do. I know him. He flicks his leg up and sends the ball flying over his head. It's a beautiful thing to see. It lands right in the corner of the goal. Their keeper lands on the ground. And the score is one to three.

Wherever Corelli's mum is in the crowd, she's doing the Mexican Wave. I'd put money on it. She's not dancing alone. Coach is at the side waving his arms around like he's at a disco. But the night is still young.

'Don't relax yet, Faltrain,' Martin warns.

But I do. And that's the great thing. I haven't felt this good in months. I'm the old me. I'm the girl who can score goals better than anyone on the field. And I'm going to enjoy every last second of this game.

The kick-off is theirs, but I know exactly where I have to be. Because I know Flemming. I've played beside him for years.

He takes possession and kicks. The ball moves and I arrive a second before their midfielder. He's good. I'm better. I run with the ball, blocking him the whole way, my arm held out for balance. I'm sailing through sky. Nothing can stop me.

'Over here,' Martin calls, and I kick to him, high over the top of the defender's head. Martin passes to King, who is already in position. He traps it with his chest, flicks it to his knee and then kicks it into goal.

Two: three.

There are ten minutes to go. We can't win, but we can tie.

Sometimes a tie is the best you can hope for. Sometimes it's all you deserve.

Woodbury is too quick when play starts again. He's as desperate as we are. And he has every right to be. Like Alyce said, sometimes there's not a bad guy. Sometimes there's just another side. He's flying down the field, so fast that no one can catch him. He's in the middle of one of those golden moments, you know, the sort you only have once in your life. If he kicks this we can't even tie. There's no way.

Martin runs after him. He pushes harder than he ever has before. Even I can't keep up with him. He overtakes Woodbury by a neck near the opposition's goal and takes the ball. He changes direction quickly, light, like a bird spinning in the air. His whole body seems as though it's made of water, it moves so easily. He starts to run but there's a crowd of opposition players in front of him, ready to steal the ball, ready to fire it in for the final goal of the match. I go in behind the pack. 'Trust me, Martin,' I whisper.

Martin kicks hard and sends it into them. To anyone else it looks like he's throwing the game. But I'm the shadow near all those players and he knows it. He trusts me. I'm smaller than them. I'm faster. I'm better. I slide in and scoop out the ball. I flick it to the side where Corelli is waiting. Flemming is in position. He catches it when Corelli boots towards him. There are only three minutes on the clock.

Flemming storms up the field, feet sheeting like rain. He dodges anyone in his path. He doesn't hit back at the defender at his side. He doesn't need to. He's a second ahead of him. And he trusts that it's enough. The crowd is roaring at Flemming as he barrels along. He's faster than I've ever seen him before.

I run too. We all do. Not because we think he'll need the help, but because it's amazing and we want to be there when he kicks that goal.

He moves into the square and we spread out around him, protection in case he needs us. No one moves to interfere. He might not make the shot, but he's earned the right to decide the play.

One minute to go and a defender blocks him. It would be so easy for Flemming to take him down. He doesn't, though. 'Faltrain,' he yells, and I take the pass. He sprints out to the side, an impossible angle, but I know he can make it. In that last minute I kick it back to him. He takes the ball and sends it flying to the side of the goal. The keeper dives to his left and almost catches it. It's a beautiful play on his part, too. We score on the whistle. It's a tie. But ask any of us on the field today, on either side, and they'll all tell you that we won.

'Did you see that goal, Martin,' I'm yelling as the crowd goes wild.

'I did, Faltrain. And it was fantastic.' Our whole team is piling onto each other like the old days, screaming and yelling. Coach piles on too.

I can't help it, the sun hits Martin's face and he looks so happy that I kiss him. He picks up the soccer ball and starts running. 'Come on.' He turns to me and races across the field. He kicks the ball and I chase him. I run even though I know that today, I have no chance of catching him.

'Look, Faltrain,' Martin says after we've dropped onto the ground. I follow his eyes. There's someone talking to Flemming, handing him a card.

'He made it,' I say. And just as I do, that guy starts walking towards Martin and me.

The old Gracie Faltrain? Maybe she would have run off to meet him.

But I'm not leaving Martin today, not for all the scouts in the world.

46

Girl Scouted in Saturday's Game Along
with the Rest of Her Team.
The Daily Times

'Not bad,' I say, holding the paper while Flemming rewinds the tape of the match for the fifteenth time. 'It's a great picture of me. Woodbury looks okay, too.' I'm shaking his hand in the photo. We're holding the scout's business card up at the camera and grinning.

'Not bad at all, Faltrain,' Flemming answers. 'Where's Knight? Isn't he coming to celebrate with the rest of us?'

'He's on his way.' And he is. 'He's just going to take a little longer.'

'It's not over till it's over,' as Jane would say. You better believe it. Not in the life and times of Gracie Faltrain.

MORE BESTSELLING FICTION AVAILABLE FROM PAN MACMILLAN

Cath Crowley

The Life and Times of Gracie Faltrain

Star *noun*: any large body like the sun,
immensely hot and producing its
own energy by nuclear reactions;

Soccer star *noun*: Gracie Faltrain

Goal-kicking, supergirl, soccer star. Gracie Faltrain is on her way. To the National Championships. To Nick. To everything she's ever wanted. Or so she thinks. Gracie's about to find out that life is messy. And hard. And beautiful.

Then her best friend moves away, the soccer team want her off the field and, after an unfortunate incident at the movies involving an ear (Nick's) and a tongue (Gracie's), Gracie has become a social outcast. And that's when Gracie's parents hit her with the worst news of all . . .

Before she has time to take a breath, Gracie's rushing headlong into screwing up, making up and trying to keep it all together. Welcome to the life and times of Gracie Faltrain.

'Teenage girls will love this book . . . a resounding success'
COURIER MAIL

'[Crowley's] rapid shifts of perspective spin us around, just like the best children's books have always done and, hopefully, will always do'
WEEKEND AUSTRALIAN

'Touching and hilarious, you'll love it'
GIRLFRIEND MAGAZINE

Cath Crowley
Chasing Charlie Duskin

Charlie Duskin is running.

Fleeing from failures and memories and friends who have given up on her. And she's not only running, she's chasing things — like a father who will talk to her, friends who don't think she's as invisible as a piece of cling wrap, and an experience with a boy in which she doesn't look like an idiot.

But Charlie Duskin is about to have the best summer of her life. She's about to fall in love. She just doesn't know it yet.

Jaclyn Moriarty
Feeling Sorry for Celia

Dear Ms Clarry,
It is with great pleasure that we invite you to join our Society.
We have just found out about your holiday. It is so impressive! You had four assignments, an English essay and a chapter of Maths to do. And you didn't do one single piece of homework!
Fabulous!
Also we have a feeling that you have a History test today.
And you're trying to study now? On the bus? With the Brookfield boys climbing onto each other's shoulders to get to the emergency roof exit? And with Celia about to get on the bus at any moment? And you think that's going to make a difference!!!
That's really very amusing, Elizabeth. We like you for it.
You're perfect for our Society and we're very excited about having you join.
Yours sincerely,
The Manager
Society of People who are Definitely Going to Fail High School (and Most Probably Life as Well!)

'Elizabeth Clarry is exactly the sort of person I'd love for a best friend'
MELINA MARCHETTA, AUTHOR OF *LOOKING FOR ALIBRANDI*

'I absolutely loved it. I wish I'd written it'
MARIAN KEYES

'Moriarty's writing is a hoot and her sense of irony perfectly placed in this hilarious addition to the genre of genuinely comic Australian young adult novels'
THE AUSTRALIAN

Jaclyn Moriarty
Finding Cassie Crazy

Protest in Mr Botherit's English Class today!

Do you value your life?

Then say NO to Mr B's Ashbury–Brookfield Pen Pal Project!
WHATEVER YOU DO, DON'T WRITE A LETTER IN CLASS TODAY! If Mr B asks why, remind him that:

- *The reason judo is compulsory here at Ashbury is so we can defend ourselves against Brookfield students.*
- *You can't get in to Brookfield unless you have a criminal record.*
- *Brookfield students don't know how to read or write.*

Year 10 is pretty crazy for best friends Lydia, Cassie and Emily, and when their English teacher starts the Pen Pal Project so that they can experience the Joy of the Envelope with boys from scary Brookfield High, life gets even crazier.

As Lydia turns into a secret agent and Emily a relationship expert, it is not so clear what is happening to Cassie. She is writing to someone, but not even her friends know what's going on. Does she even have a pen pal? Or has Cassie really lost it?

The eagerly awaited, deliciously humorous new novel from the author of the award-winning bestseller, *Feeling Sorry for Celia*.